THE

PANAMA
CONTAGION

BOOKS BY DM COFFMAN

Fiction:
The Net Conspiracy

The Hainan Conflict

The Panama Contagion

The Harbin Connection (coming in 2021)

The Hainan Incident (an LDS version of books 1 & 2 in The Net thriller series)

Non-Fiction:
Above the Best: The Remarkable Life of Seeley E. Ralphs

China Through the Eyes of Her Students: A glimpse at life in China through uncensored student journals

THE

PANAMA

CONTAGION

A Novel

DM Coffman

THE PANAMA CONTAGION

Cover design by Laércio Messias at 99designs

Visit DM's website at www.dmcoffman.com to learn more about the author and her books, to participate in upcoming book plot/character development contests, win prizes, etc.

This is a work of fiction. The names, places, characters, events, etc. are used fictitiously and are not to be construed as real.

ISBN: 979-8-61643-286-5

To my family

Acknowledgments

I began this story years ago. The idea of a cruise ship virus becoming a pandemic was part of The Net thriller series from the beginning. Being one who enjoys cruising, I know the real danger of germs on ships. I understand having my hands sprayed with disinfectant by crew members when boarding, before meals, etc., and I use the hand sanitizer stations located throughout the ship whenever I pass one. I appreciate crews who keep them well-stocked. And I prefer cruise lines that take extra care to disinfect their ships while in port before boarding new passengers.

So, when it came time to finish this book, I felt pretty knowledgeable about viruses on cruise ships. One thing I thought I would have to research was the outcome such a pandemic would have on a country as passengers returned home and unknowingly infected others. Little did I know, such a scenario would play out right before my eyes as the COVID-19 pandemic hit. I can only hope it does not prove to be as deadly as my imaginary Panama Contagion.

As for all of the research done for this book, it never seemed to be enough. Thank you to those who helped. Even still, I am sure there are many flaws and errors—technical and non-technical—even for a simple work of fiction.

Chapter 1

*B*oom! The explosion propelled dozens of twenty-foot shipping containers into the air and overboard the cargo vessel. The ship's alarms blared as master and crew ran to the port side to determine what had happened. Minutes later, a succession of explosions tore through the ship's mid-section, splitting it in half. Falling debris littered the Indian Ocean for over five miles. After thirty minutes the alarms stopped. Other than the raging fire, large enough to be seen from space, and the distress signal from the Emergency Position Indicating Radio Beacon, the ship was quiet.

* * *

The SS Kodiak carried crude oil and combustible liquids. While enroute to South Korea at approximately 1500 hours and one thousand miles off the coast of Hawaii, it suffered what was believed to be major fires in the starboard fuel oil storage tanks. The explosions blew the stack deck and stack off the ship and caused extensive damage to the engine room killing crewmen on watch.

"Lower the portside lifeboat!" the master barked at the remaining crew members. "Abandon ship!"

The surviving crew and contract workers evacuated down lead lines running off the port bow into the lifeboat. As they maneuvered away from the burning tanker they watched in shock as the ship's boom swung wildly from side to side, snapping cables and demolishing the ship's deckhouse, machinery house, navigation bridge, and communications room, rendering the vessel a total loss.

Chapter 2

BRUSSELS, BELGIUM
JULY 8

The Net directors gathered as usual for their quarterly meeting. It was just after 5am on the second Sunday of the third quarter. Armed guards stood outside the locked boardroom.

"We have had some recent successes," the white-haired man began, a gleeful glint in his voice.

The directors applauded.

"I wish to commend the Foreigner for his handling of these outcomes."

More applause.

"As a result, we are now in a position to escalate our influence in preventing the US government's involvement in the Middle East."

The directors were silent.

The white-haired man continued. "Gentlemen, we must create a diversion large enough to monopolize fully the attention of the United States.

We now have that capability. Therefore, in addition to existing scheduled attacks, I propose a direct hit on the Panama Canal."

The directors remained silent. Several glanced at each other.

"Okay," one director broke the silence. "But why Panama? They don't even have a military."

"Precisely," the white-haired man stated. "Without their own military the United States would have to come to their aid. The US is not going to allow the Panama Canal to be jeopardized in any way. By attacking the canal, the United States would be forced to resume control of operations at least until repairs could be made."

"That's right," reflected one of the directors. "Although the United States turned over all functions to Panama, the stipulation was that if the canal were ever in jeopardy, the US would take back operations. Panama has no military, and ninety-nine percent of the Canal's operations have been privatized by the Panamanian government."

"Since we can assume you are talking about an attack using one of our ships, what's the possibility that the ship's identity can be traced back to us?" a director inquired.

"An excellent question," the white-haired man responded. Looking at the Foreigner, he said, "Please explain to the directors how we acquire and register our ships."

"Certainly. Gentlemen, as you may or may not know, the international maritime trade is largely unregulated. As a result, the industry loses track of many ships—not only ours but others as well—because they are frequently given new, fictitious names and then reregistered with fake corporations. Tracing a ship back to its real owner can be an impossible task, if you want it to be."

"Thank you." The white-haired man turned to face the map again and highlighted with the laser pointer the Pacific entrance to the Panama Canal. He continued, "As you know, locks are flood chambers used to lift or lower ships through uneven waterways. Without them, there is no passage. The Panama Canal has three. After being positioned into the largest, called the Miraflores, one of our reregistered cruise ships loaded with explosive cargo will be detonated, taking out the lock, the harbor crew, and a substantial portion of the canal, rendering it impassable."

"The Canal's sophisticated scanning equipment would pick up explosive cargo long before our ship could get anywhere near the canal entrance, let alone positioned into a lock," one director said, shaking his head, skeptical of the plan's viability.

"And why a cruise ship?" another interjected. "Wouldn't a less expensive cargo vessel be more practical?"

"We can handle the scanning problem with financial deals. We have several Panamanian employees who are willing—for a large sum of money, of course—to arrange for the scans to appear clear," the white-haired man replied with confidence. "As for the use of a cruise ship, they are faster than other vessels and because of their size and nature, they are less likely to come under scrutiny. And, as I will point out in a moment, the passengers may be quite useful."

"You're not suggesting we blow up a ship full of people, are you? You know I'm opposed to such action," one of the directors who was a medical doctor by trade commented.

"Certainly not," the white-haired man replied. "The ship would be emptied of its passengers at that point."

"Sir, would destroying one lock result in a large enough diversion?" the Foreigner asked. "It seems to me the United States could rebuild any damaged sections of the canal within a matter of months, if not sooner. And while the canal is impassible, land transportation systems could be used to move shipments across to the other side. You would not be preventing shipments, merely delaying them. If I'm not mistaken, the railroad that runs along the canal has been modernized and can reach speeds of up to seventy miles per hour. Although its use is primarily passenger transportation and tourism, it could easily be converted for cargo, especially since it is one of the few operations still managed by the United States. If I remember correctly," the Foreigner paused for a moment, "I believe the canal's railroad is operated by Kansas City Railroad."

"Your knowledge of Panama is quite impressive, young man. And you are probably right that hitting one of the locks along the canal would not be a large enough disaster on its own," the white-haired man remarked. "That is why there would also be attacks on the railroad; the Chagres River, which supplies the water to operate the locks; both the Centennial Bridge and the Bridge of the Americas; the military refueling stations on both sides of the canal; and both coasts of the United States."

"There is no way we could get a ship loaded with explosives into a US seaport!" a director exclaimed. "Not with the use of Vehicle and Cargo Inspection Systems (VACIS) technology for port security. There is no way we could succeed. Why, it's ridiculous to even consider it!"

Another director chimed in. "And VACIS technology is becoming obsolete. I understand the United States government now has the capability of creating a three-dimensional image of cargo carriers using something like a . . . a nuclear beam, or something."

"A neutron beam scanner," the Foreigner corrected. "It's called Pulse Fast Neutron Analysis. It reveals dangerous substances by detecting the cargo's chemical make-up."

"See? Their technology for port access is too advanced," came the retort.

"Point of fact, sir, no," the Foreigner replied, shaking his head. "Use of PFNA technology is still quite limited. In reality, most US seaports only inspect about two percent of all incoming cargo. The rest rely on a filed manifest—a written list of the cargo's supposed contents—sent twenty-four hours before setting course for the United States. So, although somewhat risky, US seaport attacks are quite possible."

"Gentlemen! Please, we are getting away from the point. If we were to attack US seaports the United States as well as international shipping communities would be on guard, which would render an attack on the Panama Canal pointless. So please, hear me out."

The white-haired man paused while the directors quieted down. "In addition to an explosive attack on the Panama Canal, I propose the use of our newly acquired contagion as part of the diversion. The virus would be released on the cruise ship with sufficient incubation time prior to the passengers disembarking back in the United States. Their symptoms would not be readily apparent until after they traveled back to their respective homes in various parts of the country—increasing exposure exponentially and making the exact point of contact undeterminable. By the time the emptied cruise ship reaches the Panama Canal, the United States will be in such a state of chaos trying to isolate the virus and determine its origin, that together with the addition of the canal explosion, it would occupy the United States' full attention. There's no doubt about it."

Smiles came to the directors' faces as they realized the plan was a good one.

"I second the proposal," a director eagerly concurred.

The white-haired man breathed a sigh. "I thought you might see things my way. Now," looking at the Foreigner he added, "how long will it take to prepare for such an operation? Careful calculations and planning are needed to ensure a successful outcome. And, given the fiasco at our communications center in Hainan, I want redundancy built into the plans—one ship out of Los Angeles and one out of Miami."

The Foreigner thought for a moment. "I would like to run some additional tests specific to destroying a canal lock the size of the Miraflores. Other than that, we have reliable dock workers at both Mazatlán and Cartagena that can handle loading explosive materials before entering Panama."

The white-haired man nodded. As an afterthought he asked, "And how are you set for finances?"

"I have secured another heroin supplier. Those shipments continue to provide more than adequate funds," the Foreigner replied with a smile.

"Then can we schedule completion, let's say, in three months?"

"We can," the Foreigner answered, nodding. "Three months would put the attack during the canal's busiest season, which runs from September to December. The most effective time would be mid-October."

"Well then, you have ample time. It is proposed that we execute these additional arrangements in mid-October. All in favor say aye."

All but one of the directors voted in favor.

Chapter 3

Yi held Sarah in his arms one last time before leaving for New York City. He had been visiting Sarah almost every weekend at Temple University where she was completing a Master of Law degree sponsored by the World Trade Organization (WTO) Judicial Training Program. She and two other judges from China had been awarded scholarships based on their performance at the training program held at the National Judges College in Beijing.

Yi and seven other judges in the program were completing three months of added WTO training at New York University. All of this was required as China received permanent normal trade status in the WTO. Of course, Yi was not really a judge. In reality, he was a Chinese American attorney who worked in Senator Boyle's office in Washington, DC. But the WTO Legislative Committee director had asked him to go undercover in China's judicial system to help put an end to the corruption preventing fair trade relations.

Yi had met Sarah at the National Judges College in Beijing. He had not wanted a relationship given his undercover work, but Sarah totally mesmerized him. He had never met anyone like her. Not only did she have a brilliant legal mind and quick wit, she was incredibly beautiful with an amazing figure and silky black hair that cascaded below the middle of her back; and he loved the way her eyes squinted when she laughed, and the cute dimple that formed in her cheek.

They had spent time together on exotic Hainan Island while she recovered from her attack by Tan Yang, the corrupt judge from Guangzhou who thought Yi was spying on him. And even though Yi was focused on his investigation into allegations of a secret terrorist cell operating on Hainan, the week with her had been perfect. That is, until she found out his true identity.

Oh, she was angry alright! He had deceived her. But, more importantly, she was hurt. He had not trusted her or known her character well enough to know that she would keep the secret of his real identity. And if there was no trust, what relationship could they have? She did not think there could be any.

Her sensible mother knew otherwise. When she traveled home to be with her family in Tibet, her mother counseled her to "take happiness where you find it." Sarah knew she had to return not only to the judicial training program, but to Yi as well.

They spent their weekends together touring Pennsylvania, New York, Maryland, Washington, DC, and areas in between. Yi even showed Sarah his apartment in Washington, DC, near Georgetown University Law School—his alma mater.

"As much as I love visiting the historical monuments of DC, I'm still drawn to the simple open spaces of rural Pennsylvania," Sarah said between bites of raw goat yogurt as they drove back from another trip to the Amish country.

"Once again it all comes down to food," Yi teased.

"What can I say? This is the closest thing to Tibetan yak yogurt that I can find," Sarah chuckled.

Now, back at Temple University, she was faced again with being apart from Yi. But this time, it would be for a much longer period of time. In a few weeks he would return to China with the other judges, and she would spend a year completing the Master of Law degree.

"It's going to be very lonely with you in China and me here." Sarah distracted herself by pushing a pebble with the toe of her shoe as they stood in the park near her dormitory.

"I thought you liked it here, Sarah."

"Oh, I do. I love being in America. This has been my dream."

"Even with all the hard work and stress you're going through for this law degree?"

"Absolutely." She looked deep into his eyes. "I love studying American law."

Yi smiled. He understood how she felt.

Looking away she added, "But now, you're a significant part of that dream. It won't be the same without you."

Yi tipped her chin up to face him. "If you stay focused as I know you will," he smiled and ran his finger lightly down her nose, "the time will pass quickly. And we will be in touch by phone and email. Trust me. The training will be over in no time." He kissed her forehead.

Sarah thought for a moment. Her brow furrowed and a look of fear crossed her face.

"You know, Yi, I'm not even sure now if I want this training to end."

Yi understood why. It had only been a week since they received the terrible news—Tan Yang had escaped. Having Sarah safe in the United States allowed both of them to put the thought of Tan Yang out of their minds. That is, until now.

"When I think about returning to China, all I can see is Tan Yang's enraged face and the gun he pressed under my chin," Sarah shivered. "I can still feel the cold metal and smell the alcohol stench on his breath." She shook her head trying to remove the image. "And how can I serve in the Hainan court with Bao as the mayor? He hates me."

"And me. But he's no longer the mayor, Sarah. And my guess is, he's a long way away from Hainan." Yi hesitated before continuing. "But you raise an interesting point."

Yi thought about what Sarah had been through—the vicious attack by Tan Yang who had tried to force Sarah to tell him information about Yi's activities to stop corruption. Tan Yang had legitimate reasons to be worried. He was heavily involved in several illegal endeavors. As a judge, he stood to lose everything, possibly his life, if caught. And now he faced attempted murder charges. His attack on Sarah had put her in the hospital in a coma for days.

"I hadn't thought about how you're going to feel going back to China—especially with Tan Yang now on the loose. I can see how frightening that might be." A foreboding feeling came over him and he paused as its full meaning grew clear. "Until Tan Yang and Bao are captured and prosecuted for their crimes, it will not be safe for you in China."

Sarah nodded with a shudder.

"These weekends with you have been the best in my life. I never thought I could be so happy. Or feel so safe. What will I do without you?"

"You're going to study hard and graduate at the top of your class." Yi kissed her lightly on the lips. He thought for a moment then added, "There's something else I would like you to do while I'm gone."

Sarah nodded.

He didn't know if she would consider it, given how busy she would be studying.

"This campus has self-defense classes. I would like you to enroll in them. Promise me you'll consider it, Sarah."

Stepping back, she tilted her head and said, "Like martial arts? You do remember that I'm Buddhist, right?"

"Yes, you're vegetarian and you don't want anything killed. I know."

"We also use a mixture of Kung Fu and meditation for spiritual and physical wellbeing." She thought for a moment before adding, "But I don't think I could actually use it to defend myself."

Yi's eyebrows raised. "You know Kung Fu? You never cease to amaze me," he beamed.

"No, I couldn't use it to hurt anyone."

"Sarah, your life could be in danger! Just go to a class and see how you feel about it. That's all."

"It just won't be the same without you," she pouted, pushing the pebble again with her shoe. "And the closer it gets to the end, the more I'm going to dread returning to China. Actually," she suddenly looked up, "and I never thought I would say this, but I don't see how I can go back."

"I know. It worries me too. At least until Tan Yang and Bao are dealt with." He paused a moment then asked, "You would consider staying here in the States?"

Sarah nodded. "If you're here, and if my family could be here, yes."

Yi thought about the legal and personal ramifications if she did not return to China.

"Look, Sarah, when the other judges complete their WTO training in New York, I have to go back with them to finish my work. But I'll be back here before you finish your degree. We can discuss this at that time. There may be a way for you to stay in the States."

Chapter 4

NEW YORK UNIVERSITY, NEW YORK CITY
AUGUST 5

"How's Sarah?" Lincoln asked Yi upon his arrival back in New York City. They were roommates along with two other judges, housed in New York University's Brittany Hall dormitory during the final portion of the WTO judicial training program.

"She's struggling a little."

Lincoln looked surprised. "With the law classes?"

Yi chuckled and shook his head. "Not with her brilliant mind. No, she's struggling with thoughts of being back in China if Tan Yang and Bao aren't caught."

Lincoln nodded. "I know. Can you believe they both escaped? Who would have thought that was even possible."

"Surely the police will apprehend them before she finishes her law degree here." Yi tried to sound optimistic. "That's still over a year away."

Lincoln's brow furrowed as Yi's last comment triggered a worrisome thought. "Yes, Yi, but you on the other hand, you could be in real danger. We go back in just a few weeks."

"I'm not worried," Yi replied, brushing the thought aside. To change the subject, he added, "So, what's in the news? I haven't seen or heard any all weekend."

"Well, for one thing, remember when I told you that China's overseas shipping industry was losing billions of yuan because of corruption?" Being a maritime judge in China, Lincoln monitored the shipping industry very closely.

"Yeah, we were freezing our tails off on the Great Wall. How could I forget?" Yi responded. "But it's what inspired us to put together that list of corruption activities by province." He thought about the complaint they filed in Beijing with China's Ministry of Justice. "It's amazing the impact that list has had, isn't it? That is the best thing to come out of this judicial training, I think."

"I suppose so," Lincoln nodded, but still seemed distracted.

"At the time, you were thrilled to file the complaint. What's bothering you now?"

"I just received this month's maritime statistical report. What upsets me is the fact that we are not seeing an increase in China's shipping income as a result of that complaint," Lincoln lamented. "I really thought we would see a drastic difference by now. Especially with the sudden increase in US shipping disasters. China should have had an increase . . ."

"What did you say?" Yi interrupted.

Lincoln looked puzzled.

"What US shipping disasters?" Yi asked.

"The explosions on July 4th."

"How do you know this?"

"The maritime statistical report tracks and publishes percentages of shipping business, disasters, and other things, by country. In the last month, the United States has had an unusually high percentage of shipping disasters, especially on July 4th. Several ships had explosions so severe there were no survivors. One was so large the fire could be seen from outer space."

"Really? What would cause such a catastrophe?"

"Any number of things. Putting the wrong chemicals next to each other in cargo holds, mislabeled goods, equipment malfunction, human error," Lincoln explained.

"Yeah, but is it common?"

Lincoln shook his head. "No. In fact, because the United States has higher standards than most countries, normally their disaster statistics are lower than average. This sudden increase is very strange."

Thinking back to Hainan Island and the Net's computer screens displaying Pacific Ocean shipping lanes, Yi wondered if the disasters could be deliberate attacks. *But the Net's communications center was destroyed. Could the Net have other facilities? Ross Pomero, Director of Intelligence & Analysis at the CIA would know.*

Lincoln studied Yi as he appeared deep in thought then said, "I would think you would be more concerned about China's shipping statistics than the United States'."

"Of course," Yi lied in order to maintain his cover as a Chinese judge. "I was just curious."

Lincoln smiled and patted Yi on the back. "It is a fascinating subject, isn't it?"

Yi nodded. "Lincoln, could such a disaster actually be a staged attack?"

Lincoln thought for a moment. "Absolutely. But it's unlikely that it could be proven."

* * *

Yi phoned Ross Pomero at the CIA. After holding for a few moments, the director came on the line.

"This is Director Pomero."

"Director, this is Jason Yi."

"Yes, Jason." Muffled voices and paper shuffling sounded in the background. "Uh, how are things?"

"Fine, sir. I was wondering about the recent explosions on American cargo ships in the Pacific and Indian Oceans. In light of the Net's threat to shipping channels, what's the possibility that those explosions were actually Net attacks on US ships?"

"That would be classified information, Jason. I'm not at liberty to discuss such matters."

"Sir, given the information I extracted in the Net's communications center on Hainan, I strongly believe there's a connection."

Pomero paused as if contemplating Yi's words. "What I can tell you is that we have received no intelligence to support your theory. I'm sorry."

"Sir, is there any way this could be looked into?"

"I don't see a need for it, Jason. Let me remind you that you are still undercover in the WTO Judicial Training Program. You should be focused on keeping up your cover and continuing to be successful in that mission. Aren't you due to complete the training soon and return to China?"

"Yes, sir. We leave on August 18th."

"Very well, then. Keep up the good work and let us know if you uncover any other corruption activities there. It's really good talking to you, Jason, but I'm late for a meeting."

Before Yi could say anything more, Pomero hung up the phone.

Chapter 5

Jiaoshi Bao had been in hiding since his arrest on Hainan Island and his subsequent escape. As mayor of Sanya, he was the one who allowed the Net to set up a communications center and bioweapons lab there. They paid him handsomely and he took advantage of every corrupt opportunity. That is, until Yi discovered the Net's facility hidden in the private island that Bao's family owned called Wild Boar Island. In the chaos that followed the American's explosive destruction of the Net's center and capture of those involved, Bao had managed to escape. His connections and hidden assets provided the means for him to allude authorities.

Part of those assets included Net-sponsored massage parlors. Bao and his business partner, João Araújo, owned thirty parlors throughout southern China. For Araújo, it was merely a side venture to his more prominent casino business. He owned the Grand Casino on Macau—where he lived and put all of his efforts. He was Bao's partner in name only as arranged by his friend, Xabian, known as the Foreigner.

Xabian disliked Bao. Yes, he was a useful pawn in Net operations, but Bao was a repulsive person with no style or class. His ostentatious suits, while tailor-made, were garish and an embarrassment to Xabian. He hated being seen with him. Bao also had no boundaries. He would stoop to the lowest level of sniveling idiot if he thought it would increase his importance. And he could not be trusted because of his big mouth and his stupidity to act on his own; like arranging the plane crash of American embassy workers. That action had not been approved. The Foreigner was livid. It was why he suggested the partnership with Araújo—to distance himself from Bao as much as possible, and to have someone close by to keep an eye on him.

For Bao, the massage parlors were his lifeblood. His promotion skills and foreign connections resulted in substantial profits. Much higher than his competitors. Most of which he skimmed off the top. His parlors were unique because they specialized in human sex trafficking. Bao provided his patrons with whatever they wanted—any age, any color. And in China, the preference was Caucasian children. But once they attained a certain age or lost their usefulness, they were transported into Siberian

Russia and sold into unknown European slave markets by way of Harbin—the capital of the northernmost province in China and the world's coldest big city. Cold arctic air blowing across Siberia into Harbin required bundling up in bulky layers of heavy clothing with no exposed skin, making it easier to transport people across the border using fake documents.

Upon his arrest Bao was removed as mayor of Sanya. So, the massage parlors became not only his main source of income but also his sanctuary. He stayed hidden from authorities by moving between parlor locations.

Xavi, the newly appointed Foreigner, contacted Bao with good news. He was finally going to receive the most-coveted tourbillon watch—the symbol of the Net's organization. Xavi arranged a small ceremony at one of Bao's parlors in Shenzhen. He brought the watch and a bottle of fine baijiu liquor. A variety of dim sum and vegetables were served as well.

"I only wish this could be done in a more formal ceremony with guests," the Foreigner said as he handed Bao a small glass of the room temperature liquid. "But, given your current predicament, it is best that we keep this private."

"It is unfortunate," Bao sniveled, conceding yet not hiding his resentment for not receiving the proper recognition he felt he deserved.

"My brother, Xabian, did not see your value or your potential." Xavi placed his hand on Bao's shoulder. "Now that I am in charge of Net operations, I wish to acknowledge your great accomplishment and successful business."

"Thank you. I am honored and grateful for your acquaintance," Bao crowed, inflected with his nervous whiny laugh.

"*Ganbei,*" the Foreigner raised his beverage in a toast.

They both emptied their glasses.

"Very nice," Bao praised the Foreigner's choice of Moutai—the finest baijiu.

"I'm especially intrigued by your parlors' unique offerings," the Foreigner said. He then paused and scratched his head in disbelief. "It's genius, really. It sets your business apart from all others. I am in awe how it is you are able to acquire Caucasian children."

"I am fortunate in that regard," Bao boasted and extended his glass for the Foreigner to add more.

"And the Net benefits as well," the Foreigner said as he poured, "in our mutual businesses here and in foreign trade markets in Europe. Human trafficking adds greatly to the Net's profits with very little overhead."

"Hah!" Bao countered and took a big swig of liquor. "Maybe for you," he clucked his tongue and poked the Foreigner's chest with his finger, "but my suppliers cost me a lot in overhead!"

"I'm sure they do," the Foreigner conceded with a smile. "We must have a discussion soon when you can enlighten me about your suppliers."

"A trade secret, I'm afraid." He squinted his eyes in a snarky grin.

"Someday you may tell me," the Foreigner replied in a playful manner. They both knew full well he could easily make him say anything he wanted.

"I doubt it," Bao snapped back.

"On the other hand," the Foreigner bargained in a more serious tone, "I may be able to help you reduce those costs. In any case, it is an honor to award you the Net's prized tourbillon watch."

Bao quickly opened the case and took out the watch. One eyebrow raised as a slight frown creased a corner of his mouth. It was not the rare jackpot version that Araújo had been given, but it was a great honor, nonetheless.

"I never understood why Xabian withheld the watch from me. Especially after all I did in setting up the Net's Hainan facility."

"Well, that is now in the past," Xavi smiled.

"I hope I never have to deal with your brother ever again," Bao remarked sharply.

"I can guarantee you that will be the case," Xavi snickered as he thought back to killing his older brother. The exhilarating memory brought tiny beads of perspiration to his forehead which he quickly wiped away with his handkerchief. His father and the other directors had not cared how the killing was handled, they just wanted it done swiftly and cleanly after the botched conflict at Hainan. The Net had lost millions of dollars in facilities and trained recruits as well as in precious time, and they blamed Xabian for all of it.

Bao could not wait to show off his expensive new watch. At the very least it was worth a hundred grand. Well, maybe sixty; but he would tell everyone a hundred thousand US dollars. He knew it went against Net policy to discuss business with outsiders, but Bao knew the impact such an award would have on his peers—especially the new mayor of Sanya.

"Yes, it is quite an honor. Presented by Xavi, the new Foreigner, himself," he boasted to the new mayor as he held out his arm. "Well worth giving up my position here, which was to your advantage now that you have taken my place as mayor. You see, all of my efforts have paid off. And I even managed to keep your involvement secret from authorities when so many others were being arrested," he added with his annoying nervous laugh.

"We did have a nice arrangement here with the Net," the new mayor nodded thoughtfully. "Although they are gone now, tourism is still growing rapidly. I am grateful to you for this opportunity."

"Well, I will not expect much in return. As long as my massage parlors in Sanya continue to operate without government interference. That is all I ask."

"Of course. They certainly are doing well with the increase in tourism at Yalong Bay resort. Foreign tourists are coming from all over the world."

"My parlors' unique offerings bring them in," Bao boasted.

"Along with the beautiful scenery and luxury accommodations. Yalong Bay is becoming a second Hawaii, you know."

* * *

"I ran into your son at the Sanya bank the other day," the woman reported to Meijuan, Bao's mother, who was the leader of the primitive Li-ren tribe near Sanya. She bore the customary facial tattoos marking her as a leader.

"What has he done now?" Meijuan asked, although she was afraid to hear the answer.

"Nothing wrong. Apparently, he was honored recently for his business dealings. He was showing off an expensive watch they bestowed upon him. He referred to the man as the Foreigner, I think."

Meijuan cringed. She knew the reputation of the Foreigner and his willingness to kill anyone who got in his way. But what was really disturbing to her was the fact that if the Foreigner was bearing business gifts, it meant the Net organization was still in operation.

I wonder if Yi knows, she thought.

Meijuan had been against her son's illegal activities since he let the Net set up operations in the cave of her private island called Wild Boar. Fortunately, she had been able to get the information into the hands of an honorable Chinese American man in Beijing named Yi. He notified the American authorities who sent in secret military operatives to destroy the Net's operations. They were successful; but, unfortunately, her son had escaped punishment for his involvement.

Because of Yi's work, Meijuan was able to return to her tribe and resume her leadership role. She owed it to him to relay the information of Bao's award.

I only wish I knew what they were planning.

She went to a nearby internet café and typed in the email to Yi:

> *Dear friend,*
>
> *I am enjoying being back with my people on Hainan. I have you to thank for that, and I can never repay you enough. This enjoyment comes with great displeasure, once again, of my son's misguided activities. I have recently learned of an award he has received from the Net organization. Apparently, they are still in operation, although from what I can tell it is not from this area. I am sorry I do not have more information, but I am afraid*

*many people continue to be in grave danger
as long as the Net still exists.*
    Best regards,
    Meijuan

Yi received the email while at work at the Guangzhou administration building. The content was disturbing, but not surprising. Yi quickly keyed in a response:
    My dear Meijuan,
    I am so pleased to hear from you, but I'm dismayed by the contents of your email. The watch that your son received represents the characteristics of the Net organization. The gear mechanism, which operates freely and independently in its highly accurate precision, is the Net's symbol—the same one that was on your letter in Beijing warning us of their planned attacks on Americans. I will certainly follow up on this information.
    Your friend,
    Yi

There was only one person Yi felt he could talk to about what the Net might be planning. He too wore the honored tourbillon watch. Yi had met him by chance as they were scheduled to board the same flight off Hainan Island—the flight that shortly after take-off mysteriously crashed into the South China

Sea killing everyone on board—mostly American expats and their families from the embassy in Beijing. Yi felt a bond had formed between the two of them as they both had the good fortune to change planes. Yi had not communicated with the man since the incident. And given all the loss that the Net had experienced during the Hainan conflict, Yi could be risking his life by contacting the man now. But it was a risk he had to take.

Chapter 6

GRAND CASINO
MACAU, CHINA (SOUTH CHINA SEA)
SEPTEMBER 28

Two large doormen dressed in black tuxedos stopped Yi at the entrance of the Grand Casino of Macau, one of the finest and most luxurious casinos on the peninsula. Macau was the only area in China allowed to conduct gambling. Left over from its days under Portuguese authority, it was a lucrative industry seven times larger than Las Vegas.

"I'm here to see Mr. João Araújo," Yi stated.

"Your name?" the doorman asked with indifference.

"Yi Jichun."

The man placed a call on his cell phone, holding his empty hand over his other ear to block the loud music and background noise coming from inside the casino. A few moments later he closed his phone and nodded to Yi.

"This way," he said and tilted his head toward the door.

As they walked through the elegant gaming area of the casino, Yi could not help but be impressed at the state-of-the-art facility. Rows of machines blinked with a kaleidoscope of colorful lights, but the usual clanking sounds of coins were replaced with rhythmic beeps of electronic money transactions, and the lack of lingering cigarette smoke meant an expensive air filtration system.

As they reached the office doors, Yi took a deep breath in anticipation of coming face-to-face again with this gentleman—someone he assumed to be involved with the Net because of his unusual watch. He hoped all this man knew about him was that he was a judge in the Guangzhou administrative court who had also vacationed at the Yalong Bay resort when this man had. They met on the bus heading back to the airport and after exchanging pleasantries they swapped business cards. They later saw each other in the airport when they changed flights. They had not seen each other or had contact since then.

João Araújo met Yi at the door to his massive office. He seemed genuinely happy to see Yi. Apparently, he had not been impacted by the conflict in Hainan, or at least had not heard from Bao of Yi's involvement.

"How are things in Guangzhou?" Araújo asked. He gestured for Yi to have a seat while he returned to his chair behind his desk. He was elegant and professional in his demeanor, dressed in an expensive sharkskin suit, pleated dress shirt and stylish silk tie—quite the contrast to the casual linen attire he wore in Hainan. Yi wore his usual black suit, white shirt, and black tie—the uniform of China's judges, along with the little red pin worn on the left lapel.

"Quiet for now," Yi replied with a smile. "I just returned from the States completing the WTO judicial training. I expect things will start to pick up shortly."

Araújo stared at Yi for several moments.

"Seeing you brings back some unpleasant memories," he finally said as he continued to stare.

Tiny beads of perspiration began to form on the back of Yi's neck. Maybe it had been a mistake coming here.

"Mr. Araújo, I'm sorry if . . ."

"Please, call me John," Araújo interrupted.

"Okay, John." Yi relaxed somewhat. "I'm sorry if my visit causes any discomfort."

Araújo took out a pack of cigarettes and offered one to Yi who shook his head. Araújo took one and lit it before responding. "No, no. I am happy you came to see me. It's just that the last time we met we were about to board a plane that ended up at the bottom of the South China Sea." He exhaled. "Seeing you brought back that realization—that's all."

"Yes, I know the feeling. But it is good to see you again."

"It was fortuitous for both of us that we changed flights." Araújo thought for a moment, his brow furrowing. "I'm just sorry others were unable to do so."

Yi nodded. "It was unfortunate."

Yi watched Araújo carefully for his reaction while he added, "you know that the crash was . . . deliberate." He posed it almost as a question, wondering how Araújo could be involved with the Net and not have known they planned to crash the plane. Glancing at Araújo's left wrist, he noticed the Net's trademark tourbillon watch was still there.

Araújo flicked his cigarette a few times before answering. "I suspect the mayor of Sanya—a rather ruthless gentleman by the name of Bao—arranged the crash to have me killed."

Yi's eyes widened. He had not anticipated that response. "Bao wanted you killed?"

Araújo seemed surprised by the answer. "You know Bao?"

Yi leaned back in his chair, thinking carefully about his words. "Do you remember the storm that caused the plane to be delayed?"

Araújo nodded.

"I had been out on a rented boat in the bay and apparently the boat owner was worried when I didn't return in a timelier manner. The mayor happened to be talking with him when I returned to the pier. He introduced himself and chastised me for being out on the water while a storm was brewing." Yi chuckled and shook his head as if remembering the incident for the first time.

"Yes, I remember that day. Bao had come to the resort to drop off a business report for me."

Yi watched Araújo for his response to his next statement. "I saw him again several days later. I was having dinner in the resort restaurant when he and a very distinguished foreign-looking gentleman came in. Bao introduced the man to me. He referred to him as the Foreigner, but I believe his name was Xabian. He wore a watch very similar to yours." Yi nodded toward the tourbillon.

Araújo's face lit up. "Yes! My dear friend, Xabian."

Yi hesitated, concerned that this meeting might not have been such a good idea after all. "So, how do you know him and Bao?"

"Bao and I are business partners, I'm sorry to say." With a wave of his hand Araújo corrected his statement. "Actually, my friend Xabian arranged the partnership, but Bao and I are not close. Bao has his shops and I have mine. I am not fond of his business methods, so I try to avoid him as much as possible. As does Xabian. . . . Or I should say, did."

"Why do you say that?"

"Because Xabian no longer answers my calls."

"You've had a falling out?"

Araújo shook his head. "No. I'm afraid there's more to it than that. Xabian's brother has taken over Net operations as the Foreigner . . ."

Yi interrupted, "If I may ask, why is he referred to as the Foreigner?"

"Ah, yes," Araújo smiled. He leaned back in his executive chair and lightly tapped his fingertips together. "The organization wishes to remain anonymous to outsiders. So, they use the title instead of any names. I, however, was a close friend with Xabian."

"I see. And this Net organization is who the Foreigner works for?"

"Yes. His father runs the show. So, his brother, Xavi, would only take over if Xabian were no longer in the picture. My guess is, the Net terminated him."

"You mean they fired him?"

"No. Most likely they killed him."

Yi's eyes widened. "What kind of operation kills off a blood relative?"

"A very ruthless one I'm afraid, and something I will not easily forget. I suspect Xavi did it, and I believe my dear friend Xabian may have suffered greatly in the process."

"Why would you think that?"

Araújo slowly snubbed out his cigarette. "The family has a long history of violence. It is part of their culture. And they take punishment very seriously when they have been wronged. Xabian killed when it was necessary and when it served a purpose, but it was something he did not enjoy doing. Xavi, on the other hand, has a reputation of killing for pleasure. And from what I understand, he can be highly creative in finding ways to cause a great deal of pain before it's over."

"That is disturbing on so many levels."

Araújo nodded. "I would not want to be his target."

Yi was afraid to ask the reason why the Foreigner had been terminated, assuming it had to do with the conflict in Hainan, and all that the Net had lost in the destruction of their communications center on Wild Board Island. Yi would rather Araújo not know that he had been personally involved.

A feeling of guilt swept over Yi as he realized the impact that his undercover work had had. He hated being responsible for the death of anyone, even someone as vicious as Xabian.

Yi wanted to shift the conversation. He sat back in his chair and tried to sound as casual as possible. "I'm sure you're wondering the reason for my visit."

"Yes," Araújo responded casually. "If I can be of any assistance to you, I will do my best."

"Thank you, John." Yi smiled. He hoped the lie he was about to tell would sound convincing. "We're having some problems with a shipping carrier in Guangzhou—not operating up to code, that sort of thing. I noticed their logo is similar to your watch's symbol, so I thought I would see if there was a connection; and if so, ask if you might be willing to answer some questions about them."

"The Net's logo is very unusual," Araújo began. "And it does tie in with this watch," he added, tapping his watch's crystal. "I think as I mentioned to you when we met on Hainan, the gear is one-of-a-kind. The Net models its operation after the tourbillon gear. This particular watch—a vintage jackpot tourbillon—was given to me by Xabian after I opened my first casino here in Macau." He smiled as if reflecting on pleasant memories.

He then looked at Yi and added with a chortle, "I remember the shocked look on your face when I told you its value."

Yi joined in Araújo's laughter over his naiveté about the watch. When they first met on Hainan, Yi had noticed the unusual watch, and about choked when he learned it appraised at around $600,000 US dollars. What Araújo did not know is that Yi had also realized the gear on the watch was the same as the symbol on Meijuan's letter alleging planned terrorist attacks against Americans.

After their moment of merriment, Yi stated, "In all seriousness, John, I need to follow-up on the code violations. He then added sheepishly, "But after hearing about this Net organization, I'm not sure I want to."

Araújo chuckled. "They may be deadly if you get on their bad side, if you know what I mean. But in most respects, they operate within industry standards. If their ships aren't up to code, they need to be called on it."

Yi nodded then asked, "So, can you tell me more about their operation? Particularly their shipping business?"

"Yes, I believe so," Araújo nodded. "I know they have a training and testing facility near Bangkok in Thailand. At the north end of the pier at Laem Chabang, in fact. I have been there. That is where most of their ships in this region sail from."

Yi hesitated. He really wanted to ask how to gain access to the facility, but he knew it was not the right time.

Instead he asked, "So, have you met this brother?"

Araújo burst out laughing. "I think I've scared you off from dealing with them."

Yi nodded with a nervous chuckle, "Maybe so."

Araújo regained his composure then answered, "Not in person, although we've spoken by phone. I have to say, I'm not looking forward to meeting him face to face."

"But that is inevitable, no doubt. You are still involved with this organization?"

"Yes. I'm afraid so. But only from a financial obligation. I am not involved with any of their political activities, although Xabian did keep me informed."

Yi nodded as he analyzed what Araújo had said. *So, he's not personally involved after all. He may be of greater use than I thought.*

"I'm sorry, did you say political activities?"

Araújo nodded. "Yes, they have been known to manipulate governments and world markets when it suits their needs. I'm afraid they are not very happy with the United States right now for their involvement in the Middle East."

Yi's eyebrows raised in surprise. "They're not the ones responsible for the recent airplane attacks . . ." He tried not to appear overly concerned.

Araújo quickly waved his hand. "No, no. That was not their doing."

Yi shook his head. "Such a tragedy."

He was tempted to question further for information about other possible attacks, but he knew he needed to change the subject to avoid suspicion. Dwelling on an American tragedy might cause Araújo to doubt Yi's motives. Afterall, why would a judge from Guangzhou care about planned attacks against the US?

"And what about their involvement with China?"

"They have business dealings throughout China. As long as government administrators work with them, it's a good relationship."

Yi thought about the number of corrupt officials who had been identified in the complaint filed in Beijing. *How many of them were tied to Net activities?* he wondered.

"Well, I hope I don't run into any trouble resolving this shipping issue," Yi feigned concern.

Araújo smiled and shook his head. "I doubt it."
As an afterthought he added, "But then, with Xabian
out of the picture you may have to deal with Xavi. I
have not heard from Xabian for . . ." he paused as if
counting then leaned back in his chair and said, "at
least five months. And Xavi's extremism seems to be
the direction the organization is now going; I'm sorry
to say."

"Well, I would certainly like to resolve this issue
without dealing with Xavi." Yi nervously ran his
finger along the inside edge of his shirt collar. He
wished his tie didn't feel so tight. He paused, then
asked the real reason for his visit. "Do you think
there's any way I could take a look around their
facility in Thailand?" He hesitated, then added,
". . . Privately?"

Araújo cocked one eyebrow while studying Yi's
face. He then lit another cigarette, took a deep breath
and slowly exhaled.

"That seems like an unusual request for a simple
code violation."

Yi nodded as his mind raced for an answer.

"Yes. Yes, it does, John." He thought how he
could best explain. Maybe the truth would work. "I
just think it's the best way to get the answers I need
at this point."

Araújo nodded then thought for a moment.

"Xabian did give me a tour there once. As a
memento he gave me one of the workers' hard hats."

He reached into his desk drawer and took out what looked like a hard baseball cap. It had the Net's logo on it—the symbol that had been on Meijuan's letter.

Araújo extended the hat to Yi.

"Wear light gray coveralls and this hard hat. If you keep your head down, you should be fine. If they ask who hired you, say Xabian did at the beginning of the year, and that you've been training aboard the ship *Panamera* since then."

His eyes seemed to bore right through to Yi's core. He took another puff of his cigarette, exhaled, then added with utmost seriousness, "Be very careful, Yi. You have no idea what you could be getting yourself into."

Chapter 7

The Net's testing and navigation training facility at Laem Chabang—a port just east of Bangkok, Thailand—had taken over Net operations since the Hainan conflict. High explosive demolitions testing was staged there and then taken out to sea to be discharged. One of the projects currently in the testing phase would determine the type and number of explosives needed to maximize destruction of a cruise ship within a canal lock. Unfortunately, human error caused an accident resulting in damage to one of their cruise ships while in port.

In addition to explosives testing, Net recruits trained at the facility in cruise ship command and navigation then practiced on cruise lines operating in the South China Sea between Hong Kong, Manila, and Laem Chabang. Once these recruits became proficient and received their certification, they commanded ships crossing the Pacific to ports along the western United States, Mexico, Central America, and northern parts of South America.

Unlike other terrorist groups that infiltrated freighter crews and seized cargo ships for terrorist activity, the Net owned many of its own cargo and cruise ships. The Laem Chabang port was the main hub for Net shipping operations.

Yi arrived in Thailand using his US passport. He exchanged currency then left the Bangkok international airport. He carried a gym bag with a false bottom for his Chinese passport, identification papers, and US currency. The bag also contained gray coveralls and the hat Araújo had given him. He checked into a nearby hotel, changed clothes, and hailed a cab to the north end of the Laem Chabang pier. He exited the taxi a block before the pier and walked the remaining distance.

The acrid smell of burnt fuel oil and charred wood stung his nostrils. As he entered the dock area, he could see why. The remains of a damaged cruise ship laid dark and silent against the upper end of the pier. It tipped slightly on its side exposing a massive black hole, obviously the victim of an explosion. Further down the dock, another cruise ship and several cargo vessels bustled with the usual dock activities of loading and unloading.

Near the cruise ship several soldiers in camouflage uniforms walked along the pier with sniffing dogs weaving among rows of luggage and pallets stacked with boxed supplies. Trollies lined up waiting to take disembarking passengers to the terminal. Near the cargo ships several Terex container movers transported cargo boxes like they were small toys, moving them between the ships and the dock's storage area further in from the pier. Rows of freight containers stacked four high looked like a shipping graveyard, where lost boxes were never seen again.

Semi-trucks lined up waiting for huge forklifts to place a cargo box on their flatbed trailers before driving off.

Yi located several buildings with the Net's logo on them. He selected one, then went inside. Plain doors lined both sides of the hallway. Yi could hear voices from inside the rooms, but the low volume muffled the sound beyond understanding. One door was slightly ajar. A training class appeared to be in session. Yi moved closer and cocked his ear to the opening.

". . . The navigation and safety bridge is manned twenty-four/seven by the Senior and Chief Staff. Bridge Watch changes every four hours and consists of three people at a time. The Officer on Duty is responsible for the bridge during his watch. At the center of the bridge is the Main Workstation. The NACCOS45 is an integrated radar system with multi-pilot and chart pilot. This navigational chart console displays wind direction, speed, air pressure, relative humidity and dew point . . ."

Yi moved to another door and quietly turned the nob. Opening it just an inch, Yi could see that it was another classroom with training going on. As the instructor spoke, Yi glanced around the room observing the mannerisms and dress of the students.

". . .The 70,000-ton ship is powered by 4 main propulsion engines and maintains its arrival schedule down to the minute . . ."

Yi watched as the students scribbled copious notes.

. . . Security and fire safety include sensors at zones around the ship and water-tight compartments with automatic doors. Fire patrols are situated throughout . . ."

All but two of the students were young males. Some appeared Chinese, some Filipino, one or two Indian; but many of them appeared Middle Eastern.

". . .In addition, closed circuit cameras are strategically positioned, particularly at the entrance to the bridge. A doorbell at the bridge's entrance triggers cameras to record when someone enters, or attempts to enter . . ."

The students were all dressed the same: gray coveralls and the Net hard hat.

". . . The chart room is controlled by regulations for port authorities and ports of call. Weather reports from the surface analysis gauge are sent every six hours to and from the ship. Ship communications are monitored at all times by VHF channel 16 . . ."

Suddenly, one of the other doors flew open and a worker came charging out. Dressed in gray coveralls and one of the Net's hats, he was an Asian male, possibly Thai. Yi estimated his age to be mid-twenties.

"And don't come back here unless you're sober!" a voice shouted from inside the room.

The man muttered something in English. Yi caught the words "not my fault" as well as the smell of stale beer on the man's breath as he rushed past him and kicked open the door. Yi followed the man outside.

"Excuse me?" Yi said.

The man turned and shouted, "Now what?"

"Ah, I'm new here. I wondered if you could answer a couple of questions?"

The man seemed to calm down somewhat. "You got a smoke?"

"Sorry, no."

The man let out a breath of foul-smelling air and shoved his hands into the pockets of his coveralls.

"Was that the main office you just came out of?"

"Yeah, but I wouldn't go in there right now. The manager's got a bee up his butt."

"I got that impression."

The man studied Yi for a moment then said, "I haven't seen you around here."

"Like I said, I'm new. Spent the last six months on the *Panamera*."

"Oh, yeah? What's your area?"

"Communications."

The man nodded then looked down at his shoes, checking the bottom right sole, which appeared to have a hole in it.

"My name's Yi."

The man looked up. "Panit Anyamani."

Yi nodded. "Nice to meet you, Panit."

Afraid he would leave, Yi added, "Any chance you could give me a quick tour around here?"

Panit thought for a moment then shook his head. "Nah. I'm out of here."

"Then can I buy you a drink somewhere?"

That caught his attention.

"Sure."

"You pick the place."

The man nodded and started to walk away. Yi followed.

"So, what's your line of work?" Yi asked.

"Demolitions."

"That sounds interesting."

Panit half-chuckled. "You better know what you're doing, or it's a short career."

"Is that what happened back there?" Yi tilted his head toward the blackened cruise ship.

"That wasn't my fault," Panit retorted. The edginess returned to his voice.

Yi knew to back off.

"Just curious. Trying to get a feel for the area, that's all."

"You ask a lot of questions."

They walked the rest of the way in silence.

The bar was a small dive located in an old warehouse a block from the pier. A couple of neon beer signs hung on the outside wall, providing the only indication that liquor might be available. The word "Mannie's" was stenciled on the door.

They walked inside. Cigarette smoke hung thick. A few people sat on stools at the bar.

"Hey, Panit," the bartender called out. "I thought you were told not to come back here."

Panit raised his middle finger at the bartender.

He laughed. "What can I get you?"

"Your best imported beer. My friend here is buying."

The bartender nodded at Yi and asked, "And you?"

"Coke."

They sat at a table near the wall. A sign above them said "Toilet" with an arrow pointing to a nearby door.

The bartender brought their drinks and Yi paid in local currency.

Panit took a long swig off the bottle.

"Okay, now you can ask me questions."

It did not take long for Panit to put away several more beers. And the more he drank, the more he volunteered information.

"So, what happened with that cruise ship explosion?" Yi asked.

"It wasn't supposed to blow until it was out to sea. The detonation device wasn't wired properly. It went off prematurely."

Yi nodded as if he understood.

Panit continued, "But I didn't do the wiring on that job."

"Then why did the manager blame you?"

"The calculation of C4 was off as well," he explained. "I got the concentration ratio wrong. Instead of blowing up the ship it just blew out the starboard side."

"It seems like that's a good thing since it went off in the harbor."

"Well, they don't see it that way. An error is still an error. And in demolitions, you don't make errors."

"This may seem like a stupid question, but why blow up a cruise ship anyway?"

Panit looked at him as if he had two heads.

"You have been away, haven't you? Three months ago, we got the directive to escalate cruise ship testing in preparation for the canal lock attack in October. Where have you been, man?"

"At sea, remember? I have a lot of catching up to do." Remembering the US ships that had mysteriously exploded, Yi asked, "What about those US cargo vessels in July?"

A big grin crossed Panit's face.

"I did good, didn't I?" he bragged. "One explosion was so big, astronauts saw it from the space station!"

Other dock workers began entering the bar. Clearly a shift change had occurred and happy hour was starting. As more people began drinking, the mood grew livelier.

Fellow workers came over and spoke to Panit. He introduced them to Yi. They pushed tables together and began an evening of boisterous conversation and drinking. They took turns buying rounds for the group. They liked that Yi was cheap, only ordering Coke for himself. Especially since he was willing to take his turn buying rounds of liquor.

Yi learned the duties of the other workers. One worked in demolitions with Panit, three were forklift drivers, and one—a female—worked in the main office.

"How do you keep track of everybody?" Yi asked the girl. Her name was Kamon and she was a programmer with a degree in computer science.

"We have an IBM zSeries900 mainframe running Linux."

"Here at the dock?"

Kamon nodded. "There's a clean room between the office and the laboratory."

"There's a laboratory here too? What's it used for?"

Kamon shrugged. "My clearance isn't authorized, so I've never been in there. But I see workers in hazmat suits enter and exit. I assume it has to do with the explosives testing."

Yi whistled. "Sounds like some serious stuff."

Kamon nodded.

"And you're in communications?" she asked Yi.

"Yep. I spend most of my time onboard ship. I had a few days leave so I thought I would come check out home base. I hired on out of Guangzhou, so I've never been here before. It is pretty impressive. Maybe tomorrow you'd show me that mainframe and laboratory area."

"I guess so. It's usually pretty quiet in the afternoon after the manager leaves."

The conversation grew louder as people tried to talk over one another and as the liquor took greater effect.

Gesturing with his hands and puffing out his cheeks, Panit mimicked a big explosion.

"It's going to be huge!" he bragged.

Several other people in the bar took notice.

His demolitions co-worker, a middle-aged man named Intan, tried to stifle Panit's exuberance. "Hey, Panit, cool it, will you?"

"You just wait and see," Panit rambled on, "We're going to become world famous." Starting to slur his words, he added, "I bet they even give us one of those 'fancy' watches," putting the word fancy in air quotes.

"You need to be careful what you say, Panit. We're not supposed to talk about plans out in the open like this. You don't know who might overhear," Intan whispered.

"Hey, we're all friends here," Panit stood up from his chair. He grabbed the table's edge as he started to sway. He raised his beer. "I propose a toast. To all who witness our Halloween blast of the Panama Canal—enjoy the night's fireworks!"

As he sat down, he added with a smirk, "At least until you die." Turning to Intan, he added, "Do you think it'll be televised? I would love to see a cruise ship explode while in a canal lock. The devastation will be spectacular."

"Shut up!" Intan hissed in his ear.

Yi had heard enough. The realization that the plans he had seen outlined on the Net's computer system in Hainan might actually happen, left a queasy knot in his stomach. He needed fresh air.

Looking at his watch, he announced to the group, "It's been a long day for me, I think I'm going to head out."

Panit stood and patted Yi on the back. "See you tomorrow." He belched. "If I make it."

Another eruption of boisterous laughter broke out as Yi left the building.

"Do you even know that guy?" Intan whispered to Panit.

He circled his finger in the air as if the name would come any moment. "That's Yi," Panit said proudly then smiled. "He buys good beer."

"Have you ever seen him on the docks before today?"

"No. He said he'd been at sea."

"Come on, Panit. You know nobody is hired and gets assigned a boat without training here first. We've been around for five years and I've never seen the guy before. Something isn't right. I didn't see an ID tag on him either."

Panit shook his head. "I forget my tag all the time. That's nothing."

Intan thought for a moment. "Yeah, you're probably right."

"He does ask a lot of questions," Panit slurred. "But I like him."

A look of concern crossed Intan's face. "What kind of questions?"

"I don't remember. He wanted a tour of the place."

"See? The guy has never been here before. Something is not right. Tomorrow you better have Kamon look him up in the records. If he's not in the system, you have her contact the Foreigner. You cannot afford to screw up anything else. You're lucky they haven't fired you already."

Before returning to the hotel, Yi stopped at an internet café and sent an email to Ross Pomero at the CIA. It read:

I have verified the July US ship explosions as deliberate by the Net. An attack is planned on the Panama Canal on Halloween night. Cruise ship explosion in the locks. That is all I know for now. I will be back in Guangzhou in three days. Only email contact until then. Yi

* * *

The next morning Yi returned to the dock, but there was no sign of Panit or the other workers. He entered the same building as he had the day before. The hum of training sessions droned on through the closed doors the same as the day before. He went into the office to see Kamon.

"Good morning," he said with a smile.

"Is it?" she replied in a sullen tone.

"Seems pretty quiet around here."

"It usually is after a night of drinking. A lot of hangovers make for a quiet morning."

"I see. Good. How about that tour?"

"I'm sorry, refresh my memory? Remember, I was drinking last night too."

"You were telling me about the IBM mainframe here and the clean room between the office and the laboratory."

"Oh, yes. Sure." She took a key from her desk drawer, stood up, then opened the door at the back of the office.

"Come on." She gestured for Yi to follow.

The room was a small staging area with racks of white coats and shelves with packets of hair nets and shoe booties. She put on a white coat, cap, gloves, and shoe coverings. She handed Yi a set of the same items.

"Put these on."

As Yi dressed, he noticed a tag hanging from one of the white coats hanging on the rack. It looked like a man's ID tag. It had the word Laboratory on it.

Kamon opened the door to the clean room. The loud hum of the mainframe computer and the circulating air pierced the silence. She stepped up onto the paneled hollow floor. Yi followed.

She signed in on the computer screen on a table inside the door. Either from her hangover or not caring, she made no attempt to hide her keystrokes. Yi noted the logon code she used.

"This seems like a lot of protection for just a mainframe," Yi strained to speak over the machinery noise.

Looking at the back of the room he could see why. Along both walls were shelves lined with containers marked as hazardous chemicals.

"I take that back," he muttered under his breath.

Taking a closer look, some of the chemical names disturbed him. It had been a long time since he'd had a chemistry class, but he recognized not only ammonium nitrate, acetone peroxide, and ammonium chlorate, but also azidoazide azide, PETN, and RDX chemicals used in high explosives.

And on the back door in red lettering was the word Laboratory and a variety of caution signs.

"They do a lot of explosives testing out in the ocean," Kamon said when she noticed Yi reading the chemical labels.

"It's hard to imagine Panit handling this stuff," Yi commented, shaking his head.

Kamon laughed. "I know. But he's considered quite an expert."

Yi also noticed a large container of agarose gel—the substance used in petri dishes.

"Why would explosives testing need petri dishes?"

"I don't know," she shrugged.

"I don't think they do. So they must use this lab for biochemicals as well."

"I believe so. Last April they moved some stuff here from another lab. Apparently one of their other facilities was destroyed. But like I said, I'm not authorized; so I've never been inside that room. I couldn't tell you what they do or don't keep in there."

"Wouldn't you like to have a look?"

She hesitated then looked at her watch. "Um, I probably need to get back to my desk now."

"Sure. Sure," Yi replied, eager to put distance between himself and such highly explosive chemicals.

After removing all of the protective wear, Yi thanked Kamon and left the office.

Now to check out those other buildings.

Chapter 8

TESTING AND NAVIGATION TRAINING FACILITY
LAEM CHABANG, THAILAND
OCTOBER 10

The Foreigner arrived at the port of Laem Chabang in a foul mood. He was annoyed. Seething, in fact. Word had gotten back to him that one of the dock workers blabbed about the Net's plans to bomb the Panama Canal using a cruise ship. He suspected it was the Thai demolitions guy who had a drinking problem. It would not be the first time. He had been warned at least once about sharing company secrets. Plus, he was a lousy demolitions expert. *One of Xabian's guys*, the Foreigner thought, leaving a bitter taste in his mouth.

No, this time word was that "the problem" was a communications guy—Chinese, newly hired, who had just returned from being at sea for the past six months. *Another one of Xabian's hires no doubt.*

When he came into the office, he tossed a gym bag he had brought with him into a nearby chair. The seldom used piece of furniture sat in the corner next to a plastic palm tree—the only items of color in the otherwise drab white room.

"Where is this new guy?" he snapped at Kamon.

Before she could answer, he removed his black leather jacket and threw it over the gym bag. He wore Kiton dark denim jeans neatly creased and a black silk Zegna polo shirt.

"I haven't seen him since Friday," she replied, almost in a whisper. "I assume he shipped out again. He said he only had a few days of leave."

The Foreigner wiped the beads of perspiration that had formed on his forehead with his handkerchief, the finely stitched letter X in white silk threads turning slightly gray. A five o'clock shadow darkened his olive-complexioned face. His frown indicated that he did not like her answer. He then moved toward the gym bag as if he had forgotten something.

Kamon's eyes followed his muscled arms while he transferred something from his gym bag to his jacket pocket. She liked looking at him. But he also scared her.

"Well, track him down," he growled. "I'm too busy for this nonsense."

As an afterthought, he added in a calmer tone, "And book me a reservation in an hour or so at that international golf course, would you? You know the one."

Grabbing his leather jacket, he rushed out of the office. As he rounded the corner of the building, he saw Panit Anyamani leaning against the wall having a smoke.

"Well, well," the Foreigner grumbled.

Panit snarled back, "What brings the great Foreigner to our humble operations?"

"You're lucky it's not you this time. I'm looking for the new communications guy."

"Yi? He's gone."

"What, gone on break? Or gone for good."

"Shipped out. Which you ought to consider doing."

The Foreigner smirked at Panit's joke.

An idea then came to the Foreigner causing him to lighten his tone. He could use Panit to send a valuable message.

"Why such harsh words?" the Foreigner oozed. "Surely we can be on friendlier terms than this. Let's at least have a drink together."

"As long as you're buying." Panit tossed down his cigarette and walked over to the Foreigner.

"Where's your car?" the Foreigner asked, putting on his jacket.

"We can walk."

"I would rather we take your car."

"Okay." Panit took the keys out of his pocket and the Foreigner followed him to an old British Ford sedan. They drove the block to Mannie's bar.

"Don't turn off the engine," the Foreigner said as he got out of the car. He reached into his pocket as he walked around to the driver's side. He gestured for Panit to roll down the window.

Curious as to why the Foreigner wanted him to leave the car running, he angled his head out the window.

With a swift swipe, the Foreigner's knife blade made a slice across Panit's neck. A shocked look of horror filled his eyes.

The Foreigner grabbed Panit's jaw and through clinched teeth sneered, "Stick out your tongue."

Panit immediately responded by extending his tongue, as if obeying might make the nightmare end. The Foreigner yanked and with one rapid motion severed the tongue completely off, then dropped it in Panit's lap.

Panit's throat screamed in shock and pain. His heightened reflexes contracted causing his foot to press hard on the accelerator. His car careened into the side of Mannie's bar, crashing through the thin wood-planked wall and plowing into anyone within its deadly path.

The Foreigner smiled at his clever handiwork.

That will send a powerful message of the consequences for anyone disclosing Net secrets.

He wiped the blade and sleeve of his jacket with his handkerchief, the fine silk letter *X* now covered in blood. He then walked back to the office thinking about the championship golf course that awaited him.

Chapter 9

BRUSSELS, BELGIUM
OCTOBER 14

The Foreigner arrived in Brussels confident about the quarterly meeting. He was prepared to give a stellar status report. Operations had been running smoothly and plans were slightly ahead of schedule. He had enjoyed his visit a few days earlier to the docks and overall felt extremely pleased with himself.

It came as a shock when the white-haired man pushed him into the corner, his face flushed red with anger.

"What did I tell you about names?" he whispered inches from the Foreigner's face.

The Foreigner kept silent as he scoured his brain for understanding.

"Word got back to me about your meeting with Bao. While I accept you presenting him with a tourbillon watch, you are not, I repeat not, to be on a first-name basis. Not with anyone, you hear me? Especially not Bao, that blabbermouth. You are to be referred to as the Foreigner at all times. Have I made myself clear?" the white-haired man hissed. "We must avoid names in order to maintain anonymity!"

"I understand, sir. I am sorry. It won't happen again." The Foreigner wiped the beads of perspiration from his forehead. He had never seen such anger from this man. The sudden change of personality was disconcerting and worrisome. *Was his father losing control?*

"Let's begin," one of the other directors interjected, taking charge of the meeting. "Firstly, I want to know about the September 11th airline attacks. Who ordered them and why?"

"They were not our doing," the Foreigner replied, trying to regain his composure.

The white-haired man had settled down somewhat. He let out a sigh and a smile formed on his lips. "The September 11th attacks, while not carried out by Net operatives, have added greatly to the success of the Net's mission. They could not have come at a better time, adding further chaos for the American government to deal with. Now is the perfect time to strike at the Panama Canal."

"I wasn't aware that outside groups were planning such large-scale attacks," another director said. "Don't we lose some of our power if we aren't the ones in control? Especially if we are not even aware of what other groups are doing?"

"We are informed of many other activities. At least from the groups large enough to make a difference," the Foreigner replied.

"Like what?" the financial director asked.

The Foreigner thought for a moment. "Off the top of my head, . . . for example, . . . like the planned attacks on US warships in Indonesia by suicide bombers. Or guerrilla activity in the southern Philippines where several rebel groups are involved in kidnapping. And there's the Muslim rebellion in Thailand . . ."

"Those are small potatoes," the white-haired man discarded them with the wave of his hand. "We don't have time for this," he added with disgust.

"As directors, we need to be given this information," one director voiced concern.

"I agree. I think we need to know ahead of time what these other groups are doing."

"I disagree," the white-haired man stated.

The room fell silent.

"I did not agree to this organization becoming a dictatorship," a director's voice broke the silence.

"This is nonsense!" the white-haired man shouted and slammed his fist down on the table.

Several of the directors persisted.

"I think we should be informed of outside activity. Those September 11th attacks were massive and well-planned. Whoever executed them could interfere with our plans."

"I agree with him," another director commented.

The financial director added, "We've certainly done our share of interfering. Such as freezing over £11million in financial assets in Great Britain and $20million in Swiss accounts and other Euro banks to manipulate oil pricing . . ."

"Stop!" the white-haired man stood and screamed, his face turning bright red.

The medical director moved quickly toward him and encouraged him to sit back down. He went to the sideboard and poured a glass of water.

"Let's not fight amongst ourselves," the medical director stated calmly. "This serves no useful purpose. We must stay focused on our mission. If we deviate or become distracted by everything else going on in the world, we'll surely fail."

"Agreed," several directors chimed in.

"Yes," others concurred.

"What is the status of our existing plan?" the medical director asked.

The Foreigner stood to make his presentation.

"The Panama attack is a Go with some minor adjustments." He cleared his throat before continuing. "In order to conduct simultaneous explosions on both sides of the canal, the explosion in the locks will have to be from the Pacific side only."

"But I wanted attacks from both sides!" the white-haired man shouted. "After the fiasco at Hainan, I insist that we build duplication into our plans!"

The medical director raised his hand to quiet him down. "Please, let's stay calm."

The Foreigner nodded. "Ships only pass through the canal one direction at a time. From the Caribbean side, they pass during the day. From the Pacific, they pass at night. All ships are cleared out before the change is made. While this is occurring, ships waiting to pass through the canal line up at each end."

The white-haired man shook his head in resignation but remained quiet.

"So," the Foreigner continued, "there will be one cruise ship in the locks at the time of the explosion. It will be enough, I assure you."

"And the other explosions?" a director asked.

"Simultaneous explosions will occur at the refueling sites on each side of the canal. Igniting the stored fuel will cause greater damage to the areas and should make the canal totally impassable. We also have positioned explosives at several points along the railroad."

"And at US seaports?" the white-haired man asked.

The Foreigner paused before speaking. "So far, our stored supplies have been detected after placement and then confiscated."

"No identifying markers can be traced back to us, I hope," a director interjected with concern.

"No. We've just lost a lot of inventory is all."

"That's disappointing," the financial director complained.

"You must keep trying," the white-haired man insisted.

"Yes, I will," the Foreigner assured him.

"And the contagion?" the medical director asked.

A broad grin came to the Foreigner's mouth. "Yes, the contagion. I am on my way to Cartagena, Colombia, to deliver this precious cargo." He held up a small black case. "I have the contagion carefully packed and ready for transport. I will leave when this meeting is over."

The directors let out a collective gasp of awe.

"May we see it?" one eager director asked.

"Of course." The Foreigner then put on latex gloves, opened the case, and lifted one of the six vials from its holder.

"I think that's enough," the medical director waved with caution. "Please, let's keep those vials safely contained."

"Of course." The Foreigner put the vial away and closed the case.

"Where will distribution of the contagion occur?" a director asked.

"This is where your redundancy comes in, sir," the Foreigner smiled, looking at the white-haired man. "The contagion will be administered on at least two ships—one leaving Panama bound for Los Angeles, and the other leaving Panama heading to Miami."

Chapter 10

The Krause family waited in the registration line outside the Miami cruise line terminal along with hundreds of other people. The line did not seem to be moving, and the sticky humid heat from the lack of shade should have been intolerable. However, nothing was going to dampen the spirits of these vacationers bound for Los Angeles through the Panama Canal on the cruise ship *Antavia*.

The Krause children, eleven-year-old Danny and six-year-old Melissa (Sissy), looked for ways to entertain themselves during their wait.

"If that lady's skin was green," Danny whispered to Sissy, "she'd look just like the Grinch!"

He burst out laughing.

She snickered and nodded as he pointed out the woman in line several yards behind them. Her squinty eyes, turned up nose, and wrinkled round cheeks were a dead ringer for the Grinch. Danny wiggled his fingers like the Grinch in Sissy's face, causing her to run off, which she frequently did anyway. Their dad had to chase her down and bring her back to where the family waited in line. This was a regular game with her.

Finally, the ship was cleared to board and the passengers began making their way up the gangway onto the ship. They stopped for a family picture, then proceeded to the boarding area where people were getting their hands sprayed with sanitizer. Glasses of juice or champagne were then handed out.

"Wow," Sissy said, her eyes wide, as they passed under a sparkling giant chandelier hanging in the main foyer. She broke free and skipped off to look at it from a different angle.

Danny ran ahead to push the elevator buttons.

Other families stood waiting for the elevators. One little girl caught Danny's attention. She was about his age and very cute in a bright yellow sun dress and gold sandals. But it is what she was doing that caused him to take notice. She had long black hair, all done in tiny braids. Each braid had gold beads at the ends, and she was swinging her head back and forth causing her hair to swish and the beads to tinkle as they bounced across her shoulders.

"Hi," Danny spoke to the girl, unsure what to say. "I like your hair."

"Thanks," she responded and continued to swing her head.

"Is this your first cruise?" he asked.

She stopped swinging.

"No. We cruise a lot. What about you? Is this your first?"

She started swinging again.

"Nah, we went on a big ship a long time ago. Before my sister was born," he said pointing to his sister who was running in circles.

"Where'd you go?"

"Umm," Danny could not think of what to say. He couldn't remember where they had gone. *Somewhere starting with Can . . . ?* He had no idea. He just remembered being on another big ship.

"I think Can . . . sas?"

She burst out laughing and stopped swinging.

"Big ships don't go to Kansas."

"Oh. Then it was Canton."

"You mean Cancún?"

"Yeah, that was it," he said sheepishly.

"You're funny," she added with a big warm smile. "What's your name?"

"Danny."

"I'm Jemila."

Danny nodded then looked away. Introductions were so awkward.

Several elevators pinged and the crowd shifted toward them as the doors opened.

"Maybe I'll see you around the ship."

"What's your room number?" she asked.

Danny took the packet of card keys from his mom's hand and looked at the cabin number.

"947."

"Okay. I'll see ya." She waved and gave him a big smile.

Her family managed to fill the last space on the open elevator. Danny's family shifted toward another one as more pings sounded.

Danny saw Jemila again when his family went for the muster drill. He felt stupid in the bulky orange life vest. Some people were just carrying theirs. He was relieved to see Jemila wearing hers too. She waved.

"You want to do some exploring after this drill is over?" she asked.

"Not with this thing on," he replied, pulling on the vest.

"Just give it to your mom to take back to your room."

"Oh, okay. Sure."

After the drill finished, a vestless Jemila met up with Danny. "Come on, I'll show you around."

Danny handed his vest to his mom and the two of them set off to explore the ship.

"Where do you live?" she asked.

"In Atlanta. How about you?"

"Chicago."

"And is your school on Fall Break this week too?" Danny asked.

"Yep. This is my family's favorite time to travel. We do a cruise this time every year."

"Wow. You've probably been to a lot of places then," he said with awe. "And is that your grandma with your family?"

"Yes. She always travels with us. She lives with us now in Chicago, but she's from Nigeria."

"Is that why she dresses that way?"

Jemila laughed. "Yes, she wears the traditional Yoruba dress and headwear."

"I like it. It's very colorful." Wanting to change the subject, he asked, "So, where are we going?"

"I thought we would start by checking out the teen club and game room. Then maybe see what's on the top deck."

"My dad said there's an aqua park with pool slide up there. I definitely want to check that out. And the basketball court."

"Sure."

After exploring the top deck, Danny asked, "Did you know they have a jail on this ship?"

"You mean the brig?"

"Yeah, the brig. Who do you think they put in there? Is it, like, for bad guys who might attack the ship or something?"

"Maybe," she replied and thought for a moment. "I hadn't really thought about it. I would love to see it though, wouldn't you? They also have a morgue. Did you know that?"

"For dead bodies?" Danny was shocked.

"Yep."

"I thought they dumped the dead bodies into the sea. Like in the movies, ya know. All wrapped up in cloth like a mummy."

She laughed. "You're crazy. They keep dead bodies in the morgue on ice until they stop at the next port."

"Wow, you know so much." But then he wondered if she was making it all up, so he asked, "How do you know all this stuff?"

"I ask the crew. And once I took a tour of the staff and kitchen areas. Did you know there's a big wide hallway that runs the whole length of the ship? That's where the workers run up and down between jobs. They call it the highway. And they have escalators between decks, like in the kitchen areas." Jemila loved sharing information.

"They give tours?"

"Sometimes," she said as she swung by her arm around a pole.

"I would love to see that."

"We'll check the schedule."

Danny thought for a moment before sharing his concern with Jemila. She seemed to know about everything. Maybe she would know the answer to what was worrying him.

"Do you think there's a possibility of a pirate attack?" Danny blurted out the question that had been weighing heavy on his mind.

"Or that the ship could sink?" he added, trying not to seem overly concerned.

She giggled. "I really don't think so."

Two officers in white uniforms happened to walk by them.

"Let's ask," Jemila said.

"Excuse me," she addressed the officers and practically jumped in front of them, causing them to stop.

"Yes?" one of the officers replied. His name tag read Vikram Padilla, 3rd Officer. He had one stripe on his shoulder. The other man's tag said Nino Temones, A/C Engineer.

"We have some questions about the safety of this ship," Jemila spoke very grown-up.

"Okay," the officer named Vikram responded. "What do you want to know?"

"Well, for one, could this ship sink? You know, like the Titanic?" Danny asked.

"There aren't any icebergs around here," the man named Nino replied and both men chuckled.

Vikram then responded in a more serious tone. "But any ship can sink under the right circumstances. That's why we have lifeboats. You went to the muster drill, right?"

"Yes. But what if there's not enough room for everybody?"

Vikram put his hand on Danny's shoulder.

"We have enough lifeboats for every person on this ship plus hundreds more. It's required by law."

"Really?"

"Yep," the officer replied and started to move forward.

"Well, what about a pirate attack?" Danny asked. "We're going to be in the Caribbean. Aren't there a lot of pirates there?"

"Not in a couple hundred years," Vikram responded with a laugh.

"Argh," Nino mimicked and elbowed Vikram in the ribs.

"But what do you do if the ship is attacked?" This was a real concern for Danny, and he needed answers. "Do you keep weapons onboard?"

The officer could see that Danny was genuinely worried.

"Is this your first cruise?" he asked.

"Second. But it's been a long time since the first one. I don't remember a lot about it."

The officer nodded in understanding. "Well, I can assure you this ship is very safe. We don't keep any weapons onboard, but if we think there may be a dangerous situation, sometimes we have Navy SEALs on the ship, and they have weapons. Or, we radio for help from any number of military battleships in the area."

"There are battleships in the area?" Danny responded in awe, his eyes wide.

"Absolutely."

"And they would come if we were attacked?"

"Within minutes."

"That's so cool," Danny breathed out, clearly relieved. The idea that military forces would come in an instant calmed all of his fears.

But that raised another question in his mind. With a puzzled look on his face, Danny asked, "Then what's the brig for?"

In his most serious voice, Vikram replied, "That's for kids who ask too many questions."

Danny froze and his eyes shot wide open before he realized the officer was joking with him. He and Jemila burst out laughing.

"Have we answered all of your questions?" Vikram asked.

"I think so," Jemila replied.

"Thanks, sir!" Danny beamed a big smile and saluted.

Both officers saluted him back then left, pleased that they had alleviated the fears of a young passenger.

Turning to Jemila, Danny exclaimed, "Let's go get some ice cream!" Now that he could stop worrying about the ship's safety, he was going to enjoy himself.

Chapter 11

The Foreigner boarded the cruise ship *Antavia* at Cartagena—the last stop on the Caribbean side before entering the Panama Canal at Limon Bay. The ship would then pass through the Gatun locks, travel through Gatun Lake along the Chagres River crossing through the Pedro Miguel and Miraflores locks to the Pacific Ocean side, then dock at Panama City before continuing on to Los Angeles, stopping only at the port of Mazatlán where the Foreigner would disembark.

In addition to a suitcase, the Foreigner also carried the small black case containing the vials of the deadly virus.

"Welcome aboard, sir," a senior officer said to the Foreigner as he checked him in. "Would you like someone to show you to your cabin?"

"No, I know my way around. Thanks."

The Foreigner put the keycard in his pocket and headed toward his cabin. He had a few days to kill before arriving in Mazatlán. He planned to study the layout of the canal and surrounding areas as the ship passed from the Caribbean side to the Pacific Ocean. He wanted to see firsthand how the canal operated, the movement of ships through, the layout of the land and waterway. And he would envision how the Net's explosions would impact the areas. The anticipation filled him with a sense of power and excitement.

The next morning the cruise ship cleared entrance to the Atlantic side of the Panama Canal. The canal crew boarded the ship and took command. The engines were powered down. The Foreigner watched from his balcony in fascination as the ship prepared to enter the first lock. Two men in a rowboat received the anchor cable lines from the ship. They then rowed to the lock's edge and attached the cables to the electric mules that would stabilize the ship through the lock.

A voice from the ship's sound system explained the process to the guests as they watched from all sides of the ship. ". . . The Panama Canal has three locks each containing one to three chambers that will raise or lower the ship. Manmade dams provide the electrical power, and electric 'push-me-pull-me' mules stabilize the ship through each lock . . ."

The first lock's gates slowly closed, and water poured in from the sides lifting the ship to the higher level. With only inches between the ship and the lock's side walls, the Foreigner watched the precision with which the process occurred.

His reverie was broken by the voice over the sound system.

". . . Passage takes eight to ten hours, which is always on Eastern Standard Time . . ."

The Foreigner adjusted his watch. Timing would be critical. He needed to meet a recruit on the dock at Panama City, who would take some of the contagion onto a ship bound for Miami.

". . . The narrowest section is nine miles along the Chagres River, which is undergoing a widening project as part of a modernization phase to increase the number of transits through the canal from 36 to 47 per day."

Soon that will be zero, the Foreigner thought and chuckled.

". . . The toll for a ship to pass through the canal is based on weight and averages approximately $75,000 to $150,000 US dollars . . ."

He quickly did the calculations in his head. *Stopping canal passage at a cost of over $4.7 million per day would exceed $140 million US dollars per month. That would bring any economy to its knees.*

As the ship made its way along the Chagres River, the Foreigner scanned the bare horizon. The emptiness bothered him. He had thought the whole canal area would be populated or constructed, so that their explosions would cause more damage. This area was nothing! *How much more is like this?* His forehead filled with beads of perspiration. He hated that trait. His father and his brothers also had the problem, but his was the worst. It seemed he was always having to wipe perspiration from his forehead or the drops would run down his face. Once again, he took out his handkerchief and wiped his forehead.

At the point he estimated to be midway, his thoughts drifted to the secret US submarine base located in the mid-area of the canal. The Net had been unable to pinpoint its exact location. Nevertheless, they had made extra provisions. Thoughts that their added explosives sites might actually take out such a military base brought cold goosebumps to the Foreigner's skin despite the hot climate. The sudden body temperature change sent a shiver down his spine, heightening his anticipation. October 31st could not come soon enough.

He watched as the parallel railroad tracks appeared then disappeared into the countryside behind dense foliage and waterways. He thought about its laser-welded seamless design allowing for high speed travel, and how the Net's strategically placed explosions would bring land transportation to a screeching halt. *But for how long?*

The solid rock sides of the Gaillard Cut and the engineering feat it took to bring about its excavation heightened his pleasure in imagining its total destruction. *It will take months to clear passage once again.* A smile creased the corner of his mouth.

But the sight that brought him the most heart-pounding exhilaration appeared while looking out over the military refueling station, American consulate, and American embassy building near the old US military base on the Pacific side. He nodded his head and beamed with pleasure as he envisioned the carnage that would soon take place. He took pictures of the areas to capture the current appearance; because very soon, it would never look the same again.

Seeing firsthand the areas that he was about to destroy, visualizing the massive carnage that he had the power to bring about, stirred feelings within him that he knew could become an addiction. And he welcomed it. The only thing that could make those feelings more intense would be to experience the destruction itself, to be there in person.

The impact of high explosives onboard a large ship in such a confined area of the locks would be massive, he thought. *If only there could be passengers onboard . . .*

Chapter 12

The *Antavia* docked in Panama City late in the afternoon on Friday, October 20th. It would remain docked until late the next afternoon. Passengers were eager to disembark and enjoy the tropical nightlife of Panama and book their excursions for the next day.

The Foreigner exited the ship and waited on the dock. The hot humid air felt particularly sticky and the graying clouds overhead indicated a storm might roll in. He glanced at his watch, 5:05pm, then shoved his hands in his khaki pants pockets and exhaled. Patience was not his strong point. He was to meet a Net recruit from the Miami-bound ship at 5:20. In his shirt pocket he carried a small black pouch with two vials of the contagion. A drop of sweat ran down the side of his face. He took out his handkerchief and wiped the annoying perspiration from his forehead. *Damn this heat.*

"Sir?" the young man called out just after 5:15.

The Foreigner recognized him and nodded.

"You have something for me?" the young man asked.

The Foreigner handed over the small pouch and replied, "You're clear on the instructions?"

"Absolutely. I'll take care of it. I've got to be back onboard by 6:00pm." His ship had arrived the day before and was scheduled to pass through the canal that evening. It would arrive in Miami in five days.

The Foreigner walked with him.

"What do you recommend for nightlife here?"

The recruit did not hesitate a moment. "Alexander's. Great beer and cigars. And girls."

"Thanks. I'll check it out," the Foreigner replied as he turned toward the pier terminal exit.

* * *

"Last call," the 2nd officer announced as the Foreigner re-boarded the ship on Saturday. "We sail in ten minutes."

The Foreigner nodded and proceeded through the ship's scanners. His head pounded from the activities of the night before. *Some aspirin would be nice,* he thought. He needed to return to his room, collect the black case, and meet 3rd officer Vikram Padilla at the crew work area aft on deck 3 at 5:00pm.

Vikram was waiting for him when he arrived.

Once inside the work area, they began filling empty spray bottles with a saline solution.

"Why Panama?" Vikram asked.

"We don't want passengers exhibiting symptoms until they reach Los Angeles," the Foreigner mumbled, not really in the mood for small talk but Vikram was critical to his plan—he had to make an effort. "This is the best location before LA." He forced a smile.

"That's five days away. What happens if some get sick before then?"

"Exposure takes about five days, so we should be fine. If some get sick earlier, most likely it will be viewed as a harmless flu bug." He shrugged his shoulders. "I wouldn't worry about it."

"Just so long as none of it gets on me," Vikram joked, leaning away and waving his hands as if terrified.

The Foreigner sprayed him with some saline solution and Vikram feigned a choking fit.

They both chuckled and it lightened the mood.

The Foreigner took out two vials of the contagion and poured equal amounts into each of the spray bottles. He then added a slight floral scent, and Vikram put special disinfectant labels on each bottle.

Vikram sniffed the container of scent and nodded his approval.

"A nice touch, don't you think?" the Foreigner smirked.

"You're a sick man."

The Foreigner frowned. "You may be right. In fact," he scratched his five o'clock shadow, an idea coming to mind. "I think I want to do some of the spraying. We are about the same size. Take off your uniform."

"What?"

"Take off your uniform." He pointed at Vikram's white officer's uniform and hat. "Take it off. I want to wear it long enough to spray some people. You can wait here or wear my clothes. I don't care."

"You really are sick," Vikram scowled as he began to remove his clothes.

As the Foreigner dressed in Vikram's uniform, out of habit he put his handkerchief in the pants pocket. When he finished dressing, he wheeled the cart to the crew distribution area.

Crew members went to their assigned posts at each dining area entrance with their bottles of the special disinfectant to spray on passengers' hands as they entered to eat. Regularly disinfecting the passengers' hands using spray bottles was a common practice to prevent the spread of viruses. But, this time, spreading a virus was exactly what the Foreigner had in mind.

He stood at the entrance to the main buffet dining area on deck 10—one of the busiest areas. So busy he did not notice two kids coming up behind him.

"Hey, Vikram," Jemila asked. They had seen the single stripe on his shoulder and assumed it was Vikram. "How many Oscars have you done?"

"What?" the Foreigner replied, startled but focused on spraying hands. "I don't know anyone named Oscar." At a lull in the crowd he turned toward the voice while wiping his forehead with his handkerchief. "What? What are you talking about?"

"Oh," Danny said with a start, "you're not Vikram."

"But your name tag says Vikram Padilla," Jemila added, pointing at the name tag on the Foreigner's uniform. "Why are you wearing his uniform?"

The Foreigner lunged toward them just as another crowd turned into the dining area. He stopped, then smiled at the crowd and began spraying hands again. Danny and Jemila ran off, fearful that the man in Vikram's uniform would harm them.

"That wasn't Vikram," Danny whispered to Jemila when they were clear of the area.

"And that wasn't any cruise officer either," Jemila replied, a stunned look on her face.

"How do you know?"

"Anyone who works on a cruise ship knows that Oscar means Man Overboard."

* * *

At the next port, in Mazatlán, Mexico, the Foreigner quietly left the ship.

Chapter 13

PACIFIC OCEAN
NEAR THE PORT OF LOS ANGELES, CALIFORNIA
OCTOBER 24

"Mommy, my tummy hurts," Sissy complained at dinner. Moments later, she threw up onto the floor. Her mother quickly grabbed her napkin and wiped Sissy's mouth. Waiters scurried to clean up the mess before it affected other passengers. Feeling her forehead, a look of concern came over Anne Krause's face.

"She's burning up," she said to her husband, Ryan. "I better take her back to the room."

Ryan nodded and brushed some hair out of Sissy's face. "I hope you feel better, honey." He gently kissed her on the cheek. Turning to his wife he added, "I'll take Danny to the show. Come and get me if you need anything."

"Okay," she smiled, then carried Sissy out of the restaurant.

When Ryan and Danny returned to their cabin, Anne was pacing the floor.

"I think she needs a doctor," Anne sputtered, tears starting to form in her eyes. "She's not able to keep any liquids down and I'm not able to get her body to cool down. I tried cool compresses. I even took her into a tepid shower . . ." her voice trailed off, helpless.

Ryan went to the phone and dialed the medical clinic.

"Yes, room 947. We have an extremely sick little girl here. She's running what appears to be a very high temperature and she's unable to keep down food or fluids." He listened then added, "She's six." He paused for several more moments then nodded. "Yes, we'll meet you at the clinic."

After hanging up the phone, he bundled Sissy in a blanket. She was limp and he could feel the heat from her body through the blanket. He kissed Anne and said, "Hopefully they can help her and we'll be back very soon."

"Danny, are you okay to stay here? I think I should go with them," Anne smiled trying not to alarm Danny.

"Sure, I'm fine."

"We'll be at the medical clinic on deck 10. You know where that is?" Ryan asked.

"Yep. No problem. Unless you want me to come with you now." Danny was worried about Sissy too.

"Okay, let's all go," Ryan smiled and tousled Danny's hair.

When they got to the clinic other people were already waiting.

"Apparently we're not the only sick ones," Ryan whispered, disappointment obvious in his voice.

"What illness is your family experiencing?" a middle-aged man standing nearby asked, who appeared to be with a woman and a teenaged son sitting on the floor holding a towel with ice to his head.

"So far it's just my daughter," Ryan responded. "She's extremely sick with high fever and nausea. We can't get her fever down or keep fluids in her."

"I've talked to most everyone here and that appears to be the case for most of us."

Ryan nodded then turned to his wife. "Anne, you and Danny go back to the room. We need to minimize the amount of exposure to the two of you."

Anne gave Ryan a concerned look. She did not want to leave Sissy, but she understood. It was best for Danny. She kissed Sissy and Ryan. Then, putting her hands onto Danny's shoulders, she steered him toward the steps heading back to their cabin.

"You heard your dad. Let's go." Anne tried to sound upbeat.

"Is Sissy going to be okay?" Danny asked, looking back at his sister wrapped in a blanket laying limp in their dad's arms.

Anne nodded, fighting tears. "Of course."

She had to stay strong for Danny.

An hour later Ryan returned to their cabin with Sissy still limp in his arms.

"Did you see the doctor?" Anne looked incredulous, taking Sissy from Ryan then sitting down on the bed with her in her lap.

"Yes. But there is no room in the medical center. They said the best place for her was here in our cabin."

"I can't believe that." Anne began rocking Sissy in her arms.

"They're asking people to stay in their cabins. They feel that is the safest thing to do. They gave me a bottle of liquid Tylenol and told me to make sure she keeps taking fluids. We are to call Room Service and order juices and popsicles—whatever they have. And we need to keep her in loose dry clothes. We can sponge bathe her in lukewarm water, but she's not to get chills."

"We have to just wait this out? I can't believe that."

"I guess so. They said it's a virus so the fever will just run its course. And that we shouldn't be alarmed unless she starts having trouble breathing."

Anne nodded as she studied the precious face of her little girl. Her breathing was shallow, but not labored. For that, Anne felt grateful.

Ryan picked up the phone and dialed room service. The line was busy.

"This is your captain speaking," a voice came over the ship's loudspeaker. "Despite every care and precaution, we appear to be experiencing an onboard virus. We are taking extra measures to prevent its spread and ask for your cooperation. We have activated Outbreak Prevention Plan level 3 which means crew members must take over the handling and serving of all foods at buffets, and all linens must be put in biohazard bags which will be carefully laundered at special facilities while in port. We will continue to disinfect surfaces regularly. But we also ask that you use the hand sanitizer dispensers located throughout the ship as often as possible and please wash your hands frequently. If you are experiencing symptoms, we ask that you remain in your cabin. Thank you."

The rest of the cruise lost its appeal for Danny. He was worried about Sissy. And for Jemila's grandma who had not been feeling well either. So, most of the time Danny and Jemila stayed with their families in their cabins.

* * *

The ship arrived in Los Angeles harbor on October 25th at 6:05am. By 10:00am Port Authority still had not authorized any passengers to disembark.

"I've notified the Centers for Disease Control and Prevention (CDC)," the port authority director said to the personnel under his command. "They will have investigators and medical specialists here shortly. Once the passengers and crew have been cleared, no one goes on or off that ship until the CDC has completed their investigation. You got that? I need everyone's best performance today."

The employees all nodded as they glanced around the room.

"Standard procedure," one of the supervisors whispered. "What's the big deal? These viruses happen all the time."

"What was that?" the director barked.

"Sorry, sir. I was just sayin' how this was standard procedure, that's all," the supervisor responded sheepishly.

"Standard procedure my ass! We've got seventeen dead bodies coming off that boat and nobody knows why. The CDC has already issued No-Sail orders and they haven't even arrived yet. Now get out of here!" The director threw his clipboard across the room. He did not need this kind of crap today.

The stunned supervisors looked at each other in silence as they scurried to leave the room.

Teams of CDC medical specialists dressed in personal protection equipment (PPEs) set up stations at the end of the gangways with digital thermometers and clipboards preparing to screen each passenger for symptoms as they disembarked and to ask where they were headed.

Danny and his mother stood on their balcony on the starboard side watching the activity taking place on the dock. Numerous ambulances and several county medical examiner-coroner vehicles pulled up and waited for the ship to unload.

Tears streamed down both Danny's and Anne's faces. Sissy had been taken to the ship's medical center during the night. She had suddenly stopped breathing and Ryan rushed her there for help. The doctor hooked her up to an IV for fluids and placed her on oxygen to help her breathe. She remained at the medical center along with Ryan, who was starting to show signs of a cough. Because of the high potential for contagiousness, Danny and Anne were not allowed to be in the medical center, and they would not be able to accompany Sissy and Ryan as they were taken off the ship and transported by ambulance to Harbor-UCLA Medical Center. Anne was instructed to gather their belongings with Danny and, once cleared by medical personnel checking all disembarking passengers, to meet Ryan at the hospital's Pediatric Intensive Care Unit (PICU) to learn more about Sissy's condition.

As Danny and Anne left the ship, other families also appeared to be in shock as they comforted each other while slowly exiting down the gangway. Many were startled by the shrill sound of sirens starting to blare as ambulances left the terminal area in their rush for the nearest hospital. Danny noticed Jemila and her family. Her grandmother was not with them. As he looked around for her brightly colored dress and head covering, he noticed several body bags being loaded into medical examiner-coroner vans. He remembered what Jemila had told him about a morgue onboard ship, and how they kept dead bodies on ice until they arrived in port. The thought sent a shiver down his spine.

"Mom, Jemila's grandma isn't with her family. Can we go talk to them? Make sure everything is okay?"

"Of course. I'd like to say goodbye to her family as well." Anne waved to Jemila's mother and started in their direction. Danny ran ahead to Jemila. She was crying.

"She . . . died," Jemila muttered between sobs.

"What?" Danny was shocked. He didn't know what to say. With all the noise from the ambulances, maybe he had misunderstood her.

"My grandma's dead," Jemila sobbed.

Anne arrived just in time to hear Jemila's statement.

"Did I hear Jemila correctly?" Anne asked Salma and Franklin, Jemila's parents.

"Yes, she took sick just a few days ago, then yesterday she was unable to breathe and late last night she stopped breathing. The doctors were unable to revive her," Franklin replied while comforting Salma who dabbed a tissue to her eyes.

"Salma, I'm so sorry! It's unbelievable how quickly this illness has hit so many people. They've taken Sissy to the hospital by ambulance. Ryan went with her. Danny and I are on our way there now."

"Oh, Anne! Not Sissy, that sweet child." Salma took out an address card with their phone number and gave it to Anne. "Please keep us informed on her health and your family. You'll all be in our prayers."

"Same to you, Salma," Anne replied and gave her a hug.

Danny gave Jemila a hug. This was the worst day of his life. And he never wanted to go on another cruise ship ever again!

* * *

After the passengers were cleared, six infectious disease specialists from the CDC's Los Angeles County Center for Preparedness and Response arrived and began taking samples from surfaces, foods, airducts and fluid containment facilities onboard the ship. Two other specialists went to the hospital and began taking samples from passengers who had been admitted. And one specialist was assigned to collect samples from deceased passengers transported to the morgue. All of the specialists were covered head to toe in disposable Tyvek jumpsuits and full-face helmets. And all samples were carefully sealed and clearly marked as hazardous.

The next day, another cruise ship from Panama with similarly sick and dying passengers arrived in Miami, Florida. The ship's morgue contained thirteen bodies. The CDC's Miami office began the same process.

Chapter 14

"The *Antavia* is going into dry dock in Cartagena, Colombia for equipment modifications. I don't see what this delay is all about." The Foreigner negotiated on the phone with a port authority supervisor named Fred. "I'll lose my docking reservation if the *Antavia* doesn't arrive by the 31st!" With an extra edge of anger, he added, "Are you going to take responsibility for that?"

"Look, my instructions are that until we know what virus or toxin is infecting your ship, you've got a No-Sail order and the *Antavia* isn't to leave this harbor. That's all I know," the supervisor responded with indifference. He had heard every excuse. These calls were a dime a dozen.

"Come on," the Foreigner pleaded. "You know it's one of any number of flu-like viruses. They happen all the time. We've even had them happen on this ship before. We always do a thorough cleaning and disinfecting—much more than required. And this time, we're not even taking on passengers. The ship will be empty except for a barebones crew."

"Yeah, that makes sense. But I can't help ya."

"Is there a fee I can pay?"

"Nope."

"Okay. So, what's the procedure? Who do I need to call to get this done?" The Foreigner pounded his fist against the wall.

"Once the CDC determines what the virus is, they will let us know what level of cleaning and disinfecting has to be done before the ship can be released. They will then lift the No-Sail order."

"That's it?"

"That's all."

"Okay. I'll get back with you."

"No, someone from the CDC will get back with us."

"Right."

The Foreigner hung up the phone. Who did he know with connections at the CDC?

* * *

Six hours later, the port authority received CDC clearance on the *Antavia* based on the following conditions: Undetermined flu-like virus. No passengers boarding. Required deep level cleaning and disinfection. Destination dry dock in Cartagena, Colombia.

"Good news," the supervisor told the Foreigner. "Once you complete deep level cleaning and disinfection, you are cleared to sail. But no passengers."

The cruise ship *Antavia* departed Los Angeles Harbor the morning of October 27th, bound for Cartagena, Colombia. The itinerary listed one stop at Mazatlán, Mexico for scrapping of internal ship furnishings, refueling, and loading of essential equipment for drydock modifications. The ship's pilot and crew were certified to maneuver the vessel through the Panama Canal. Pilot and crew would then disembark in Cartagena. Passage through the Panama Canal would occur from the Pacific side, scheduled for the evening of October 31st.

The Foreigner waited in Mazatlán for the *Antavia* to arrive. Also waiting were six large cargo crates marked "Mechanical Equipment: Fragile – This Side Up." But what they really contained were massive quantities of high-level explosives.

Chapter 15

THE CENTERS FOR DISEASE CONTROL AND
PREVENTION (CDC), ATLANTA, GEORGIA
OCTOBER 27

Normally when a virus outbreak occurs, an
emergency operations center is set up in that city as
the CDC's command center for dealing with the
outbreak. Because similar symptoms had occurred in
passengers from two different cruise ships arriving a
day apart in Los Angeles and Miami, and both ships
had been in Panama at the same time five days prior,
swab samples taken from the ships and the sick and
deceased passengers were sent overnight to the
Centers for Disease Control and Prevention's
headquarters in Atlanta, Georgia. Specialists there
would determine if the illnesses were the same and if
so, what the cause of the illness was, its source, how
it was transmitted, and what the best course of
treatment would be.

However, what started out as routine testing for what appeared to be coincidental cases of a flu-like virus suddenly became a matter of top-secret national security.

The CDC scientist scratched her head and rubbed her eyes, thinking she had misread the scanning electron microscope (SEM) specimen. She tried again, adjusting the alignment and magnification.

After two more attempts, she called for a second opinion.

"Neil, would you come over here, please?" she said to her colleague.

Dr. Neil Jackson put down the iodine dropper bottle he was using and came over to the SEM microscope.

"What's up, Wyn?"

"What do you see here?" Dr. Wynona Lomas replied, once again rubbing her eyes as if not believing what she had seen on the screen. She pointed to the unusual spikes on the cells displayed.

Dr. Jackson moved in for a closer look.

"That can't be," he said, shaking his head. "That just can't be."

He grabbed the *Known Deadly Viruses* binder from the shelf and began flipping through the pages.

Dr. Lomas leaned back in her chair, stretching from the long hours of work she had already put in, knowing how many more overtime hours this new situation was going to require.

"We'll have to run a rapid PCR test to identify the RNA coding to be sure. But I'll be damned if that isn't that bioweapon virus from . . . where was it?"

"Hainan Island," Dr. Jackson replied, reading from the binder.

"It has mutated, but it's clearly from the same strain," Dr. Lomas stated in her most clinical tone.

They both stared at each other as the sickening reality set in.

"But how did it get on cruise ships in Panama?" he asked.

Neither one wanted to think about the answer to that question.

"Wyn, you set up for the RNA coding and case definition study. I better get the director down here."

She nodded as Neil left the lab. They needed to work quickly. If they were correct, they could have a deadly pandemic on their hands.

Dr. Gordon Sanderson, the CDC's Deputy Director of Infectious Diseases, put on his reading glasses and carefully studied the lab report.

This pathogen is identified as a deadly mutated strain belonging to the large family of coronaviruses; specifically, a mutation from the virus confiscated in April 2001 from the Net organization's bioweapons laboratory on Wild Boar Island in Hainan Province of the Peoples' Republic of China (labeled HAiCo-

1). The origin of this pathogen is linked to a Russian virologist (current status unknown), believed to have developed the strain in laboratory in 1989, sharing many similarities with a deadly variation used for genocide in Iraq in 1990 (MERS), and a weakened variation recently identified in Guangzhou, China in July (labeled SARS).

*Testing the incubation time before manifestation of symptoms has determined exposure to the virus to be from 5-10 days. The case definition study identifies the occurrence of initial exposure to have occurred sometime while the two cruise ships (*Antavia and Southlandia) *were in port at Panama City on October 21. A total of 7,218 passengers and crew members were identified as possibly exposed, traveling home (with subsequent exposure to others) to thirty-one states in the United States, and seventeen countries in North and South America, Europe, and Asia (the list of specific travel itineraries and final destination areas is attached as Exhibit A). Risk of infection after exposure is placed at a high level with possible mortality rate as high as 60% among at-risk candidates.*

IMPORTANT FILE NOTE: Discovery of any variation or mutation of this virus is to be brought to the immediate attention of Ross Pomero, Director of Intelligence & Analysis at the Central Intelligence Agency (CIA), contact information in file.

Dr. Sanderson closed the report and took off his reading glasses. Other than a slight shake of his head, he gave no impression of concern for the report.

"Wynona, please label this virus the Panama Contagion, or PanCo," he said, "and add it to the *Known Deadly Viruses* binder." To both doctors he added, "Discuss this with no one until I say otherwise. We do not want to cause any alarm just yet. I need to make some phone calls."

He then left the laboratory.

Dr. Sanderson returned to his office and telephoned Ross Pomero at the CIA, on his direct line.

The response was almost immediate.

"This is Director Pomero."

"Ross, this is Gordon Sanderson at the CDC. We've got a problem."

"Okay."

"A mutation of that Hainan virus bioweapon your people collected last spring has been introduced here in the States."

"What?" Pomero shouted. "We confiscated all there was of that virus."

"Apparently not."

Pomero chewed on the corner of his lip while he thought through the ramifications of this news.

"Ross?" the doctor wondered if Pomero had hung up on him.

"Well, how bad is it?"

"Tests on the mutation indicate that it could be more deadly than the original strain."

"You've got to be kidding me!" Pomero could not believe what he was hearing. *The Hainan virus was contained—a done deal. Was the Net still in operation? If so, where?* His thoughts scrambled as he tried to assess the meaning and impact of such a reality. *Was this an act of war? A terrorist attack?* He needed more details. "What's our exposure at this point? Where was the contagion introduced?"

"I hope you're sitting down, Ross. We're talking nationwide pandemic proportions with exposure in several other countries as well. It came in on two cruise ships from Panama . . . "

"Panama!" Pomero interrupted. "How the hell did it get to Panama?"

"I hoped you could answer that."

"Not off the top of my head!" Pomero had no clue. He was still trying to figure out how the virus had survived the Hainan conflict.

"So, where did the ships dock in the US?" Pomero asked, preparing for the worst. "No place with any sizable population, I hope."

"One into Los Angeles. The other Miami."

Pomero slammed his fist down on his desk.

The doctor continued. "Our forecast models put the potential number of cases in the United States alone at 1.5 million with a conservative range of hospitalizations between 250,000 and 460,000 with an estimated death rate of 40-60%. Estimated worldwide cases could be in the millions."

Pomero began mumbling obscenities under his breath.

"How long do we have before this all hits the fan?" He was almost afraid to ask.

"Maybe ten days."

"That doesn't give us much time."

"The CDC has protocols for these types of outbreaks," the doctor stated matter-of-factly. "We just need to get them all in place as quickly as possible."

"I need to make two quick calls."

"I think we need to involve the Head of the CIA and the President of the United States," the doctor urged.

"Yes," Pomero concurred. "Let me make these two calls first, then I will set up a conference call including you, Director Stanton, and the President."

The doctor agreed. "Let's say fifteen minutes."

Chapter 16

Ross Pomero pressed the button on his console for the Southeast Asian intelligence division. "Bring up all we have on the Net organization since the Operation April Fools Hainan conflict."

He quickly scanned through the documents before placing a call to Yi's cell phone. He anticipated waking Yi up at his apartment in Guangzhou, China.

"This is Yi." Yi answered on the fourth ring, a slight hint of grogginess in his voice.

"Sorry to wake you, Jason. This is Director Pomero at the CIA."

"No problem, sir." Yi sat up and rubbed his eyes. What can I do for you?"

"I know this isn't directly related to your mission, but it's a rather urgent matter that I'm hoping you can help me with."

"Okay. Sure." Yi put his phone on speaker, reached over and turned on the light, swung his legs over the edge of his bed and sat up. Given that it was still dark outside, he looked at the time: *3:17am on Sunday, October 28th.*

"There's been a possible virus outbreak here in the States, directly linked to the flu virus found in the Net's bioweapons lab in Hainan."

Yi pushed strands of his thick black hair back that had fallen onto his forehead. "I don't understand. I thought the CIA controlled all there was of that virus." Yi was now wide awake.

"I thought so, too." Pomero cleared his throat before continuing. "We've since learned that after the island was destroyed, the Net somehow consolidated their operations to a shipyard and training or testing facility in the Indochina peninsula area. We believe that it may be located near Thailand. Anyway, Jason, somehow some of that virus found its way to Panama and onto two cruise ships that recently docked in Los Angeles and Miami."

Yi muttered something under his breath.

Pomero hesitated, unsure if asking him to get involved might turn into a fiasco. Afterall, Yi was not a trained CIA agent.

"I know this is asking a lot, Jason, but I'm hoping your research skills could be used to quickly determine where the Net might have such a facility? I'm assuming it would be near your location." He cleared his throat before continuing. "And then, . . . I know there may be some risk, . . . but if you could attempt to . . . possibly access that facility. I need to know if they have a bioweapons laboratory there."

Pomero cleared his throat again, anticipating silence while Yi thought about what he was proposing.

"That's not a problem, sir," Yi immediately replied with a yawn. "I happen to know right where their facility is and I've already been in the . . . "

"What?!" Pomero shouted. "What?!"

"It's a long story." Yi smiled at the effect he knew he was having on Pomero. "Let's just say that I met someone with Net connections when we were both supposed to be on that Hainan flight that they deliberately crashed into the South China Sea. Somehow, avoiding that fate created a bond between us."

"So that plane crash was deliberate after all?"

Yi knew Pomero hated acknowledging what the CIA had been unable to prove.

"Yes, sir. Not fully sanctioned by the Net but carried out by one of their over-zealous recruits, nonetheless."

"All those American embassy families . . . murdered," Pomero mumbled, his voice trailing off.

"In any case, sir, when you ignored my warning about the cargo ship attacks in July . . ."

"What cargo ship attacks?" Pomero interrupted; this time annoyed at Yi's arrogance in implying that he would ignore a valid warning.

"The fourth of July explosions."

"There is no proof, or any intelligence reports suggesting that those explosions were deliberate," Pomero postured with confidence.

"Sir, I spoke with the demolitions expert myself. He described with detailed accuracy how the Net carried out those attacks."

Yi could almost hear Pomero's gasp.

"You did what?! . . . Wait. . . . You better start from the beginning, Jason. How did you locate their facility, and how the hell did you gain access? And don't tell me there was an underwater entrance and you just swam in!"

"No, sir," Yi laughed, remembering how he had gained access to the Net's hidden cave on Wild Boar Island. "I contacted this acquaintance—a casino owner—because I suspected he had connections to the Net, which he did. I told him there were some Guangzhou shipping violations that I needed to clear up through their headquarters. He told me about their Thailand facility and even helped me gain access. I was there earlier this month."

"That was brilliant, Jason." Pomero scratched his head. "So it is in Thailand." Maybe Yi was a better undercover agent than he had thought or given him credit for.

"Yes. It's a shipyard and navigational training facility at the port of Laem Chabang. But they also conduct explosives testing from that facility. That's how I happened to speak with the demolitions expert. They have a crew that operates from there." Yi paused as a nagging reality set in. "Sir, I emailed you about this early in the month. More importantly, I told you in that email that they were planning an explosives attack on the Panama Canal on October 31st. That's only three days away. Certainly you've made plans to stop that attack."

Silence on the line.

"We have received no intelligence reports that those July explosions were deliberate attacks, or that this organization has any plans of attack on the 31st."

"Sir, I was there! And I saw those same plans on their computer screen in Hainan. I sent photos of those Hainan screen shots to Senator Woodbury. I'm sure he gave you copies."

"We could not confirm those photographs. Our intel does not support your findings—then or now."

Yi could not believe what he was hearing.

"If they released their virus, sir," Yi emphasized the word *sir,* "it's a good indication that they intend to execute their plans." He then paused before pointing out the obvious: "It would appear that your intelligence on this group is severely lacking."

Pomero was silent. Yi knew he had to be fuming. *Let him stew awhile,* Yi thought. *Maybe now he'll take the Net seriously.*

Pomero grumbled. "That may be the case." Clearing his throat, he continued. "All of that aside, and I can't worry about speculation on a possible attack right now, we've got this deadly virus here with possible ties to that facility. I need to know if there's a bioweapons laboratory there and . . ."

"I would say there is," Yi interrupted.

"How do you know that?!" Pomero hollered, clearly flustered by Yi's unsupported information.

"I saw the door to their laboratory at that facility. It abuts to their mainframe computer's clean room area. They store chemicals used for explosives testing, but they also store large quantities of agar substrate. They certainly do not need that for explosives testing. They would use petri dish agar only if they were also involved with biochemicals. Isn't that right, sir?"

Again, there was silence on the line. The only sound Yi could hear was the squeak of Pomero's chair.

"Jason," he spoke with renewed excitement. "This may be a long shot, but is there any way you could go back to their facility and get into that laboratory? We need to see if this virus came from there. Because if it did, and I suspect so, they may have a viral inhibitor or antigen for this virus. If they have one, or some sort of an antiviral drug from which a vaccine could be made, it would save valuable time and hundreds of thousands of lives."

Yi thought for a brief moment. "Yes, I believe I could do that. But my concern, sir, is that I have no clue what to look for or how to handle such a substance."

"Of course, Jason. I wouldn't expect you to know such things. I would send an expert to go with you. I know of an Asian lab worker here at the CIA who is perfect for the job. He's an excellent agent and highly skilled. He can extract samples and handle their transport back to the States." After pausing a moment and then as if talking to himself he added, "And their mainframe may be in that same area? If so, I would want him to try accessing their files. Maybe he could verify this allegation of a possible pending attack . . ."

Yi did not bother telling Pomero that he already knew how to access their computer.

"That sounds great, sir," Yi replied. "I'll meet your guy at the Bangkok international airport. Email me his name and the details of his arrival. Tell him to bring gray coveralls and watch for me carrying a sign with his name on it."

Yi then disconnected the line.

The second call Pomero needed to make was to his boss—the head of the CIA and Director of Central Intelligence, Mark Stanton.

"Hello, director. This is Ross. I would like to meet with you immediately. I have confirmed preliminary intelligence reports of a terrorist attack on the United States using a bioweapon virus. I have spoken with the CDC. We are in the process of verifying their findings. After briefing you, sir, I would like to set up a conference call from your office with the CDC and the President of the United States."

Chapter 17

THE WHITE HOUSE
WASHINGTON, DC
OCTOBER 27

Ross Pomero set up the conference call between himself, his boss Mark Stanton, Dr. Gordon Sanderson, and US President Stephen Bradshaw.

Director Stanton began the conversation. "Mr. President, preliminary intelligence reports and recent samples gathered by the CDC indicate that a potential medical situation may arise in certain parts of the United States. The CDC's Deputy Director of Infectious Diseases has joined us today to explain what they found."

"Dr. Sanderson, it is a pleasure to speak with you," the president responded warmly. "Gentlemen, please go on. This sounds interesting."

"Gordon, if you don't mind," Ross Pomero quickly interjected, "I would like to preface this discussion by stating that certain aspects of this dialogue pertain to a top-secret operation known to the president as Operation April Fools. Mr. President, without going into detail, do you recall this conflict?"

"Yes, Ross," the president replied, wondering where this bit of drama from the CIA was headed.

Pomero continued, "The CDC believes that a virus recently detected on two cruise ships that arrived in Los Angeles and Miami in the last few days may be a mutated strain from that conflict." He emphasized the word *may*.

"What does that mean, Ross? Your briefing at the time stated that the operation had been a success and that the CIA now controlled that virus."

"Yes, Mr. President, that is true," Pomero postured. "We have yet to verify the CDC's findings."

Dr. Sanderson cleared his throat. "If I may, Mr. President?"

"Please."

"As Director Pomero has pointed out, this virus was brought to the CDC's attention after being collected from passengers and surface and fluid specimens taken from the two cruise ships. These samples were tested at our Atlanta laboratory and the virus has been confirmed to be an unknown mutation of the Hainan strain. Because both ships were traced back to Panama as the origin of infection, this virus has been labeled the Panama Contagion."

"Thank you for clarifying, doctor. And wasn't the Hainan strain a flu virus? Is this Panama Contagion something we should be concerned about?" the president asked.

"In actuality, while many of the symptoms are similar to those of the influenza viruses, this and the Hainan strain belong to the family of coronaviruses which are much more severe. We do not have vaccines for them. And, it does appear that this Panama strain is likely to prove more deadly than the Hainan one."

"We have no proof of that," Pomero interrupted.

"Based on the number of deaths from the two cruise ships and the rapid decline in patients' conditions so far . . ."

"How many deaths?" the president asked with concern.

"Thirty-seven since the ships arrived two days ago."

"My heavens, just how bad is this contagion?"

"Well, as a comparison, Mr. President, of those who contracted the flu virus of 1918, about two percent died. Since 1997, the H5N1 virus, or bird flu, has demonstrated a forty percent death rate although transmissions are far less frequent. Preliminary models show that this virus is highly contagious, and the death rate could top 40% including high percentages among healthy young adults."

"Those models could be wrong," Pomero scoffed.

"Let's hope they are," Stanton remarked.

"In the meantime, what's the amount of exposure?" the president asked. "How many people are we talking about?"

Dr. Sanderson responded. "There were over seven thousand passengers and crew. The CDC set up screening stations at each port prior to disembarkation. Technicians screened each person for symptoms and documented travel itineraries and destinations. Even though most of those passengers were asymptomatic, they could have potentially infected others as they traveled to their final destinations."

"We don't know that for sure, since we don't know exactly how this is transmitted," Pomero interjected.

"The CDC is continuing its testing, yes," the doctor countered. "But based on what we've seen from these passengers and coronavirus characteristics in general, in all likelihood transmission is by respiratory droplets—a highly contagious scenario in a closed environment."

"We will continue to monitor the passengers and crew to see if they develop any symptoms. By doing so, we should be able to track potential outbreaks, if any," Stanton added.

"That sounds optimistic," the president responded with a lilt in his voice.

"It's not that simple," Dr. Sanderson's voice edged up in volume. "In fact, I feel that I need to emphasize the importance of implementing CDC protocols now in preparation for a potential pandemic."

"A pandemic! Come now," the president chuckled, wanting to keep the conversation from getting too serious.

"Yes, a pandemic," the doctor insisted. "Based on our forecasting models, the US could see 1.5 million cases over the next six to eight months with a conservative spike of 250,000 hospitalizations with a 40-60% death rate to over 460,000 hospitalizations. Our hospitals are not equipped to handle even a fraction of that patient load."

"Let's not get carried away," Pomero retorted trying to alleviate any tension. He thought about the possibility of his CIA agent bringing back an antigen for the virus. If that were to happen, there would be no need to alarm the public over a potential virus outbreak. The threat would be eliminated. He would be a hero.

"What are you saying, Ross?" the doctor challenged, shocked by what Pomero was now suggesting. "We discussed this earlier and we were both in agreement. This needs to be dealt with."

"I agree with Ross," Mark Stanton chimed in. "Let's not get ahead of ourselves."

"Yes," the president concurred. "We don't want people to panic. I think we ought to hold off until we know this is really going to amount to something."

"That sounds like a plan," Stanton agreed.

"This is a mistake," the doctor implored. "We are dealing with a serious and deadly virus."

"If it proves to be so, then we will deal with it. Let's give it a few days to make sure," the president announced before he hung up the phone.

Chapter 18

TESTING AND NAVIGATION TRAINING FACILITY
LAEM CHABANG, THAILAND
OCTOBER 28

Yi flew from Guangzhou to the Bangkok airport, collected his bag, then changed into his gray coveralls in a stall in the men's bathroom. He left the Net hard hat in his bag. He then proceeded to the designated location and waited for the CIA agent. He carried a sign with the name Edward Sipkema printed on it.

Edward arrived on schedule, looking refreshed and already dressed in gray coveralls. He arrived by chartered flight and passed through Thai Customs with an expedited entry. He approached Yi with a smile as if they were close friends. The strap of his overnight bag crossed his muscular chest and he carried a black briefcase in his left hand. He extended his right hand to Yi in a warm handshake.

He was not what Yi had expected, and Yi had to stifle a chuckle at his error of falling for false stereotypes. Pomero had said "Asian lab worker" and Yi had expected a small-built man with glasses and a pocket protector. This man was at least six foot two, two hundred pounds of lean muscle, with only a hint of Asian facial characteristics and military-cut black hair.

"Sipkema is an unusual name," Yi said as he looked up at the guy.

"Dutch."

Yi nodded. *That explains a lot,* he thought, remembering that Dutch men were usually tall.

"So, how was your flight?" Yi asked as they headed out of the airport.

Edward nodded and smiled. "About what you'd expect."

Yi hailed a cab and they quickly got inside.

"Should we go to the hotel first?" Yi asked.

"Laem Chabang dock—north side," Edward spoke directly to the cab driver in the Thai language.

To Yi he then spoke in English, "Let's take advantage of the time."

"You're right."

Yi handed Edward the hard hat. Given his height, it would help him to blend in if someone were to see them.

By the time the cab dropped them off at the Laem Chabang dock it was just before midnight on Sunday night.

They anticipated very few workers, if any, at the Net's facility. Some might still be at the bar nearby, which would not close until 3:00am.

When they arrived at the main building, Edward set down the briefcase and gestured for Yi to wait. He then went around the side of the building. He was gone less than two minutes.

Yi had his lock pick out and ready. He assumed Edward had gone to bypass the security system. When Edward came back around the corner and gave a thumbs up, Yi unlocked the door.

They quickly slipped inside and closed the door behind them. Yi pointed at the office door, which he assumed was locked, then entered one of the classrooms to check through the windows to see if anyone might have seen them enter. Glancing around the lighted parking area and shadows beyond, Yi did not see anyone. As he exited the room, he turned on the light. If anyone had seen them, let them think students had left study materials in a classroom.

He returned to the hallway and noticed that Edward was already in the office using a small flashlight.

Yi entered the office and pointed at the desk drawer. Edward opened it. The pass card for the clean room door was in the drawer. Edward grabbed it and they both quickly entered the prep area to the clean room. The room lights came on automatically from a motion sensor. Because the room had no windows there was no concern. Yi immediately went to the rack of white lab coats where he previously had seen at least one lab ID card hanging. Fortunately, one was still there. He tossed the coat with ID to Edward then put on a white coat himself. They both put on a cap, gloves, and booties, and Edward grabbed a pair of goggles.

They entered the mainframe area. Yi pointed to the back of the room where the laboratory entrance was located. Edward nodded and carried the black briefcase to the lab door. He took off the ID card from the coat and scanned it over the security box. The box light switched from red to green and the door latch clicked open. Edward turned toward Yi and gave him a thumbs up before entering the laboratory.

Yi took a zip drive from his pocket and placed it in one of the mainframe's USB ports. He held his breath as he entered the logon and password that he remembered Kamon using. Hopefully, it had not been changed.

He exhaled as the root directory came up on the screen. *Bless you, Kamon.*

Yi quickly scanned the home directory and shared libraries. Several folders labeled "Shipping Operations" and "Tactical Plans July thru Nov" caught Yi's attention. He opened the "Tactical Plans" file. What came up on the screen made his heart race.

As he scrolled through the pages, he recognized screens similar to the Net's communications center computer screen hidden within the cave in Wild Boar Island.

One map in particular caught his attention. The date read October 31. *That's it! Maybe Pomero will believe this.*

The major highlighted area showed the Panama Canal. Numerous locations along the canal, the train tracks, and the bridges were marked with Xs, with explosives materials listed alongside each X. A ship labeled *Antavia* was positioned on the map just before the canal entrance on the Pacific Ocean side. A label by the Port of Mazatlán, Mexico read "load explosives Oct 29."

Another label on the map made Yi's stomach turn. Next to Panama City it read "virus distribution Oct 20."

Yi glanced back at the laboratory just as Edward came through the door. A smile crossed Edward's lips as he patted the black briefcase he carried.

That's a good sign, Yi thought.

Yi gestured for Edward to come see what was on the computer screen. Edward could tell that Yi was bothered by something. It did not take him long to see why. A crease formed along Edward's brow as he studied the map and saw the date.

Yi copied the files to the zip drive and logged off the computer. He handed the drive to Edward to give to Pomero personally. They had gotten what they came for. Now they needed to put things back in place and get out of there, except for one thing. Edward pointed to several corners of the ceiling. Cameras.

Yi quickly logged onto Kamon's desk computer using the same logon. Not surprisingly, it worked. Scanning the files for security cameras, he located the folders with the correct date/time stamp and deleted them. From the time intervals, Yi could see that they would have ten seconds to exit the office before the next file would open.

They left the building, secured the door and the alarm system, and headed toward the main highway to hail a cab.

They did not notice Intan and another dock worker walking back from the bar. Although Intan had been drinking, he recognized Yi as one of two men leaving the office building. *What is he doing here?* Intan thought. *He had shipped out. Otherwise, the Foreigner would have killed him instead of my friend Panit. . . . So why is he back here now? Sneaking around at this time of night?*

"How did you know what to look for in the lab?" Yi asked Edward while they were waiting for a cab.

"Some things were labeled," Edward replied. "But the best thing to do was get samples of everything. That way we know exactly what they have here. We'll test everything back at Langley."

"And the antigen?"

"Hopefully it's in here," he patted the black briefcase. "According to the labels I think it is. But we won't know until we test it."

"So, what's your background for this kind of work?" Yi asked a little sheepishly.

Edward chuckled. "PhD in microbiology from Cornell. A real nerd. What about you?"

"Georgetown Law School, international law. UC Berkeley before that, Chinese languages."

They both laughed.

"So here we are," Edward shrugged.

They stood by the lighted highway, taking in the tropical night smells and sounds that enveloped them.

Yi liked Edward. He had not been around someone he could speak openly with in a long time. It felt good.

"But you've obviously done some field work," Yi commented.

"Some."

"Where's home?" Yi asked, glad for the chance to make real small talk.

"Fairfax, Virginia now. Originally, Vancouver, Canada. And you're from Guangzhou?"

Yi chuckled, "No." He then shook his head, "Hell no, I'm on assignment there. I was born in California and my home is in DC. I worked in Senator Boyle's office. Law Researcher."

A light seemed to go on in Edward's head.

"You're a NOC—non-official cover agent," he said it like he was referring to a celebrity.

Yi shook his head. "No. I didn't say that. I'm just helping the World Trade Organization while China gets upgraded to permanent normal trade status."

"What's your cover, I mean position?"

"Administrative judge."

Edward just nodded. "Well, Yi-whoever-you-are, it's been a pleasure working with you. Now let's get this information to Director Pomero."

Yi and Edward took a taxi to a hotel near the airport. Yi would stay at the hotel and take a commercial flight back to Guangzhou later in the morning; Edward would take the CIA's chartered plane back as soon as he emailed Pomero. Upon locating the hotel's business center, Edward sent an encrypted email to Ross Pomero with a blind copy to his boss Irving Maxwell, Directorate of Operations/Special Operations Group. It read:

Acquired samples. MORE IMPORTANT: Urgent situation. Planned explosions on Panama Canal, various locations (see map in separate email), includes ship Antavia *arriving Pacific side, evening of October 31.*

Ed

Op notes: Team operated well. Extraction time 12 minutes. NOC agent highly recommended.

"I'm sure glad Pomero will take your email seriously," Yi said when Edward came out of the business center.

"What do you mean?"

"He ignored mine when I emailed him a couple weeks ago."

Edward grunted and shook his head. "Well, if he doesn't, I know my boss will."

He reached into his pocket then handed Yi his business card. "Contact me if you ever need anything. It was a pleasure working with you."

Yi nodded. They shook hands then went their separate ways.

* * *

Beads of perspiration formed on Ross Pomero's forehead and under his collar as he read the email from agent Edward Sipkema. Thoughts poured through his mind and anger filtered in as he thought about how much he disliked Jason Yi, *or Jichun Yi—whatever his name is. That know-it-all attorney paper-pusher from a senator's office. Yes, he serves his purpose scoping out corrupt officials in China's judicial system in order to appease the World Trade Organization and Senator Woodbury. So what? We trained him, we provided his documents, and we cover his ass. He's not even a real CIA agent! No one would expect the CIA's Director of Intelligence & Analysis to take anything he says seriously.*

After venting more of his anger using some choice swear words and pounding his fist on his desk, Pomero deleted all traces of Yi's email then got back to work. Time was short. A cold clarity came over him. *So, the Net is planning an attack. In three days. How can I work this to my advantage?*

He printed out the information and map that Edward had emailed him, along with Edward's email with the op notes deleted, then he created a Top-Secret folder marked Panama Canal/Oct 31, assembled it all and headed for Mark Stanton's office.

Chapter 19

THE PORT AT MAZATLÁN, MEXICO
OCTOBER 29

The Foreigner stood on the pier and repeatedly looked at his tourbillion watch, succumbing to feelings of edginess as he anticipated the arrival of the *Antavia*. Not that he was nervous about the outcome of the impending transformation. He was not. Mazatlán was the perfect location to carry out the essential tasks at hand. Being the largest port between the US and Panama, things were easily "lost" here. Like paperwork explaining exactly what was about to be loaded onto the *Antavia*. And being headquarters to one of the largest drug cartels in the world, sales and various other business transactions (even illegal ones) could be swift and secure. Furthermore, because of the high criminal element, the right people with the right motivations could easily be found, and for the right price—ones willing to work swiftly and thoroughly without paperwork and on a cash basis. No, the Foreigner was not nervous. He was excited.

Upon its arrival in Mazatlán, five important and well-timed events would happen: First, the existing cruise ship crew from Los Angeles would disembark and enjoy an all-inclusive luxury vacation in Mexico courtesy of the Net before returning to their shipping center in Thailand. Second, salvage crews would have one day to remove whatever non-navigational or mechanical equipment, hardware, kitchenware, storage tanks, lifeboats, furniture, and whatever else was not needed to sail the vessel, to be sold off. Third, the ship would be fully loaded with explosives, stabilizers and propellants, and fuel. Fourth, the Net's demolitions experts would carefully rig the explosives with detonators and timers to be set off at the precise time. And lastly, the ship would be boarded by a new, skeleton crew—a suicide crew trained specifically for this purpose—to sail the *Antavia* to the Panama Canal for its final voyage.

Chapter 20

THE WHITE HOUSE
WASHINGTON, DC
OCTOBER 29

"This meeting of the National Security Council and guests has been convened to address a matter of urgency that must be resolved within the next two days," National Security Advisor Clark Mathews stated in the John F. Kennedy conference room in the west wing basement of the White House. Known as the Situation Room, the participants sat around the mahogany table, the room darkened except for the glow of high tech flat-paneled monitors mounted on the walls around them.

"Thank you, Clark," US President Stephen Bradshaw began. "As chairman of the council, given the involvement of US seaports and international shipping channels in this matter, I have asked Admiral Ralph Nilsson, Commandant of the Coast Guard, to attend. Thank you, Admiral, for joining with us today." Looking around at the council members he added, "And thank you all for assembling on such short notice. I have asked CIA Director Stanton to brief us on this critical situation."

Stanton stood. "A terrorist threat was recently uncovered by the CIA, involving planned explosions at numerous sites along the Panama Canal and several US seaports, on the evening of October 31st. The details are documented in this folder, of which you have a copy." He held up a beige folder stamped with red letters: CLASSIFIED.

Looking out over his reading glasses at the council members and guests, he continued. "The tactical plans of this terrorist attack do not involve a military strike. In fact, the crux of the threat involves an explosives-laden cruise ship and numerous other strategically placed explosive devices as you will see on the map. We surmise that their intent is to stop passage through the canal at the peak of the shipping season; thereby impacting the international shipping industry and the world economy."

An electronic version of the map appeared on the wall screens. Many of the council members switched from flipping through the pages of the folder to studying the electronic map.

"What do we know about these terrorists?" the president asked.

"It's the same group that we encountered during the Hainan Conflict when we took out their communications center and bioweapons lab," Irving Maxwell CIA Director of Operations responded.

"The April Fools Operation, if I remember correctly," USAF General Mitchell Waldron, chairman of the Joint Chiefs of Staff, stated. "A very successful joint military strike with China."

"And how did we come by this latest information? It's been verified?" National Security Advisor Clark Mathews asked.

"We received the information via email from one of our Special Ops agents just this morning who downloaded the files from this group's computer system. My department has analyzed the information and verified it to be accurate," Ross Pomero replied.

"I was afraid you were going to say that hot-shot undercover attorney . . . Yi, I believe, . . . with the WTO program, happened to walk in and find it," Defense Secretary Warren Stricklan interjected with a hardy laugh. "That was just the damnedest thing ever—there in Hainan." He kept shaking his head as if he still could not believe it.

"No, absolutely not," Pomero responded quickly. "This was one of our agents. His email came this morning. It's right here." Pomero flipped to the page in the folder.

"Several US ports are highlighted on this map," Vice President David Halverson interrupted, voicing concern while pointing at the electronic map.

"If I may?" Admiral Nilsson spoke.

"Please," the president replied.

The admiral explained. "We have increased security at all 361 of our deep-water ports. We continue to acquire new, state-of-the-art technology and we locate and extract devices in our ports on a regular basis. In fact, several recent attempts were made at two of these locations." He used an electronic pointer to highlight Seattle and Los Angeles. "Especially Los Angeles. It is our largest container facility. Since 9/11 we have increased our tracking of what cargo is entering US waters, and who serves on crews, as well as stowaways and individuals who appear to be surveying US ports."

"Who would have thought keeping track of stowaways would be necessary?" Secretary of State Tyler Jameson said, shaking his head in disbelief.

"How could a terrorist group even get explosives into a US port? Don't we have x-ray scanning devices?" Dave Halverson inquired.

The admiral answered. "Not everything gets scanned. Only about two percent of containers actually get inspected. Most tracking is done by the shipping manifests filed before the ship sails."

"So, a shipping container could be used as a Trojan horse to smuggle anything from a dirty bomb to a nuclear weapon into one of our ports," General Waldron commented.

"There are any number of ways," the admiral replied. "For example, we're on alert for signs of use of exotic craft for launching underwater attacks like small submarines and human torpedoes—underwater motor-propelled sleds that divers use. Terrorists can even pose as crewmen on freighters carrying dangerous chemicals, then commandeer one and slam it into a harbor."

"My god," Jameson muttered under his breath.

The admiral went on. "Coast Guard and Naval intelligence officials keep track of ships we think have questionable intentions or sketchy ownership. Now that governments are increasing homeland security against terrorism, nautical attacks are becoming more prevalent."

"We have confirmed intelligence reports that the multiple July 4th US cargo ship explosions were deliberate attacks by this group," Pomero interrupted, almost boasting.

The admiral nodded his acknowledgment of Pomero's comment then continued. "We use satellite tracking and surveillance planes, we coordinate with allied navies, seafarer unions, even informants, to track these suspicious vessels and organizations, but we can still lose track when they are continuously given new names, are repainted and re-registered under fictitious ownership. It's largely an unregulated and secretive global maritime industry."

"What can be done?" Clark Mathews asked.

"To start, since 9/11 the Coast Guard has set new rules for medium and large-size ships. Ninety-six hours before reaching a US port, they now must provide data about their cargo, and they must provide the names and passport numbers of all crew members, their ship's corporate details, and recent ports of call. This information is then tracked by computer at our intelligence facility in West Virginia."

"Getting back to this map," Warren Stricklan queried, "what's being done at these specific ports to protect against an attack?"

The admiral responded. "Security has been increased on incoming traffic both from land and sea, and we will be reviewing documents and scanning all questionable containers for the next seventy-two hours. Furthermore, at Los Angeles, Port Authority has added explosive sniffing K9 teams."

"Wasn't there a recent cruise ship incident at the port of Los Angeles?" Tyler Jameson questioned.

"A possible virus outbreak," Pomero said, nodding. "The CDC has it under control."

"The CDC is conducting an investigation," the admiral concurred.

The president spoke up. "Director Stanton and I met with the CDC just two days ago. Preliminary findings by the CDC indicate a possible connection between this virus and the one confiscated in Hainan at this group's communications center."

"That would be an act of war, if they've released a bioweapon here," the general declared.

"The CIA hasn't verified the CDC's findings in that regard," Stanton countered.

"But there could be a connection between this virus and these planned explosions. If it's the same group."

"Yes," Stanton replied.

"How bad is this virus, and what could happen if it gets out in the public?" Halverson asked.

"The CDC thinks it's more deadly than the Hainan strain, and it could become a pandemic," the president replied.

"But the CIA has not confirmed those findings," Stanton responded.

"When will we know?"

"At most a few days."

"We're still recovering from 9/11, we're facing terrorist attacks at home ports as well as the Panama Canal, and now we may have a potentially deadly pandemic on our hands?" Jameson said, his voice now raised.

The room fell silent.

"These are not just random terrorist acts. These are coordinated. This is a sophisticated group we're dealing with. In fact, these look like diversionary tactics," the general said, breaking the silence.

"From what?" Mathews asked.

The general shrugged. "My guess would be our involvement in the Middle East."

The president stood. "While we want to ensure the safety of our seaports here at home, let's not lose sight of the fact that we've got a cruise ship loaded with explosives headed for the Panama Canal. I want to authorize the CIA to send forces to stop that ship and disarm those explosives. Now."

The council members exchanged looks and nodded.

"Do we know for sure there aren't passengers on this cruise ship?" Mathews asked.

"Yes," the admiral replied, nodding his head. "The *Antavia* was cleared to sail out of Los Angeles only because they were not taking on any passengers. The ship's manifest listed a skeleton crew heading to Cartagena, Colombia scheduled to go into dry dock."

"Can we trust the accuracy of that manifest?"

The admiral nodded. "Dock authorities do an inspection just prior to sailing. No persons are allowed on or off ship from port after that point."

"But we now know their plan isn't to dry dock in Cartagena," Stricklan interjected.

"Gentlemen, I agree with President Bradshaw. The CIA should be authorized to deploy immediately its Special Operations Group (SOG) paramilitary forces to insert and extract these terrorists planning to carry out attacks on the Panama Canal and any other locations indicated, and defuse any explosive devices," the vice president stated.

"Director Stanton, we'll have that Council Directive to you within the hour. Time is of the essence," the president said as he stood, signaling that the meeting was over.

"And Irv, you know the Joint Special Operations Command (JSOC) out of Fort Bragg will help coordinate any support you may need," General Waldron offered as he stood and gathered his materials.

"And you've got the Coast Guard's help," the admiral added.

"We may need air support with air to surface missile capability, if we can't stop that cruise ship in time," Irv Maxwell commented as he stood to leave. He had a lot of preparation work to do.

"I'm sure they'd be happy to blow that boat right out of the water for you," the general responded with a smile.

Irv Maxwell seemed to be thinking out loud. "It's good the terrorists plan to enter the canal from the Pacific. Ships go through at night from that side. We'll have a better chance of getting onboard under night cover. The ship will pass under the Bridge of the Americas before entering the canal. Operatives could rappel down without detection."

The admiral whistled. "That's cutting it close, but you guys know what you're doing. Just remember, there's a fifteen-foot tide differential every five hours on the Pacific side. That can really mess you up if it catches you off-guard."

"Right." Maxwell nodded.

"Mr. President," Clark Mathews said as people were starting to leave the room. "What about the facility where these plans came from? Do we need to send a team in there?"

Irv Maxwell responded. "We extracted biochemical samples from a laboratory on their premises. Let's hold off until we know just what they've got there."

Mathews nodded in agreement and proceeded toward the door.

"Now how did you pull that off?" Defense Secretary Stricklan patted Maxwell on the back as they began to exit.

"Remember that hot-shot attorney you mentioned earlier?" Irv Maxwell replied with a chuckle.

"Yi? Of course."

"Well, he and one of my Special Ops microbiologists did, in fact, walk in and take them."

Warren Stricklan burst out laughing.

Ross Pomero, who was behind them, was fuming. This was supposed to be his moment of glory.

Once outside, Irv Maxwell pulled Ross aside and whispered, "Ed blind-copied me on that email. Seems you deleted a few things, including an email from Yi dated October 5th. You should not have overlooked that one, Ross."

Irv patted Ross's chest with the Classified folder then turned and walked away.

Chapter 21

Yi grabbed some food at the airport and went straight to his work at the Guangzhou administrative court. He kept an extra black suit, white shirt, and black tie—the judge's uniform—in his office. It was half past one. He had missed the morning schedule. At least he had sent an email to his boss stating that he was up all night with stomach sickness, and he hoped to be at work by early afternoon.

Luckily, the rest of his workday was slow because he was dead tired from the overnight adventure to Thailand. He looked forward to going straight home after work and getting some much-needed rest.

An uneasy feeling washed over him as he turned the key in the lock of his front door. *Boy, I am really beat,* he thought. Any other time he would have realized why he felt uneasy. The small stick he kept propped up against the door jamb was gone.

As he entered his darkened apartment and reached for the light switch, the sharp blow to the back of his head came swift and hard. His last thought before blackness engulfed him was *you really do see stars.*

At first Yi was disoriented, but as the dull throbbing pain intensified throughout his head, his recollection of events came flooding back. His fight reflexes jerked in response but constraints around his wrists and ankles prevented any movement. He was tied to a chair in his living room; and although the room was darkened by the night with only a hint of light coming from his bedroom, he could see that his apartment had been ransacked. And from the noise coming from his bedroom, he could tell that the person or persons were still there.

"Hey!" Yi yelled.

The noise in the bedroom stopped.

"So, the big man is finally awake," a voice spoke with disdain.

Yi recognized the voice.

Tan Yang.

He entered the living room holding the Net's hard hat. Certainly not the polished and elegant judge Yi knew from the judicial training in Beijing, now being forced to hide from authorities and having been stripped of his properties and financial accounts. Yi recognized him, nonetheless.

"What do you want, Tan Yang?"

"I want answers. . . . Like why weren't you at work this morning? You emailed your boss that you were sick. But you weren't here. . . . And why did you fly to Thailand last night? . . . . And what are you doing with the Net's hat?" he added as he held up the hard hat.

"Could we take off the ropes first?"

"I don't think so."

Yi shook his head in disbelief at Tan Yang's persistence.

"I don't get why you think my life is so interesting, Tan Yang. There are simple answers to your questions. I had a meeting early this morning at the Net's shipping facility at Laem Chabang to clear up some shipping violations they incurred here in Guangzhou. And they gave me the hat. Okay? Are you happy? I didn't realize that you were still working for the courts. In fact, I believe the Beijing courts found you guilty of attempted murder."

Tan Yang swung the hard hat and hit Yi across the face.

Yi tasted blood in the corner of his mouth. His fists clenched behind him. He could feel the anger build inside as he thought about Tan Yang hitting Sarah that same way.

"That's right, I forgot. You like to beat up defenseless people."

Just breathe. . . . He tried to calm himself. Anger was not the way to deal with Tan Yang.

"Sarah's fine by the way," Yi continued. "She recovered very nicely in a luxury suite on Hainan Island, thanks to your funds."

Tan Yang hit him again.

Sarcasm wasn't the way to deal with Tan Yang either; but Yi couldn't resist that one.

He tilted his head from side to side trying to get the kinks out of his neck. More than anything, he needed to get out of that chair. He was working on it. The edges of his cufflinks were designed to be sharp enough to cut through cording.

"Okay, Tan Yang. I've given you the answers. Now take off the ropes."

"Not yet. I want to know who you really are. . . . And who sent you here to Guangzhou."

"Boy, you're tenacious, Tan Yang," Yi said, shaking his head. "Why does it even matter now?"

"Because whoever did this has ruined me. I had a good thing going," Tan Yang's voice wavered with anger. "I must know who did this to me!" he added as he tightened his hand into a fist.

"You're obviously still well connected since you managed to escape the jail system here."

"Yes, thankfully," he said, calming down a little. "But obviously someone has betrayed me. So, I must find out who. Now tell me who you are and who sent you!" he raised his voice again.

Yi needed a little more time to finish cutting through the rope around his wrists. He would have to get Tan Yang to leave the room before he could deal with the ones around his ankles.

"I really am Yi Jichun. Really. That is my real name. And some people call me Jason. That's the truth."

"But you didn't go to Tsinghua University or work in the Beijing Haidian District Court, did you? Because no one remembers you there. I checked."

"You certainly do your homework."

"And I'm right, aren't I?" Tan Yang smirked.

Yi paused to weigh his options. And to use up more time.

"I'm right aren't I?" he repeated louder.

"Yes. You're right," Yi conceded, nodding his head.

"Ah, hah!" Tan Yang shouted. "I knew it!"

A puzzled look came over his face.

"But you know the law. Why hide the law school that you actually attended?"

"Because it was not a prestigious school," Yi pretended. "My background is from poor peasants; not sufficient to qualify for the high honor of working in the Guangzhou administrative courts." Yi almost gagged on the words as he said them, but he could tell Tan Yang was falling for them.

"That is true," Tan Yang said reflectively. "But I want to know what official set this up and why?" he added, tossing the hard hat onto the sofa.

"Those documents are hidden in the small suitcase in the bedroom. You would have to bring it to me."

Tan Yang immediately jumped up and left the room.

Yi quickly removed the rope around his wrists then untied the ones around his ankles. He then waited for Tan Yang to return, staying in position as if he were still tied to the chair.

When Tan Yang dropped the suitcase in Yi's lap, Yi punched him hard in the jaw, catching him off-guard and causing him to lose his balance and stagger backward.

As he regained his balance, he grabbed the club he had used to knock Yi out when he entered the apartment. A sinister smirk appeared on his face as he moved toward Yi.

"You are very clever to have gotten out of those ropes. My guess is you've had some special training."

Yi picked up the chair he had been sitting on and backed away, stepping over misplaced furniture, cushions on the floor, and pulled out desk drawers and debris scattered around from Tan Yang's ransacking.

"So which official?" Tan Yang asked as he swung the wooden club at Yi.

"Not one specifically," Yi replied and blocked the club with the chair leg.

Yi stumbled slightly as he tried to step over a fallen lamp. Tan Yang swung the club again, but Yi caught the end of the club between the legs of the chair and twisted.

Both the club and the chair fell to the floor.

"Don't lie. I want a name."

"How about the World Trade Organization? Or the Rule of Law?"

Tan Yang stopped as if that caught him by surprise.

He then lunged at Yi with both hands reaching for Yi's neck. As Yi leaned back to block Tan Yang's grasp, they both fell against the curtained glass door, breaking through onto the balcony.

Freeing himself from Tan Yang's hold, Yi managed to stand. He staggered back as Tan Yang lunged again, pushing Yi against the balcony railing. As they fought, the metal railing came loose from the weight of their bodies pressing against it. Then it gave way, falling six floors to the concrete pavement below. Yi and Tan Yang both went over the edge. Yi was able to hold on to the concrete ledge; but Tan Yang, after years of alcohol abuse and weight gain, was unable to grab hold and fell to his death.

As Yi pulled himself back up onto the balcony with every muscle of his body screaming from fatigue and his head still pounding from the whole ordeal, a depressing feeling washed over him at the thought of yet another person dying because of him.

Chapter 22

Sissy Krause laid in an isolation room of the Pediatric Intensive Care Unit (PICU) at the Harbor-UCLA Medical Center in a heavily medicated state. A plastic tent dwarfed her small body with tubes and wires coming out everywhere providing all of her nutritional and bodily needs, monitoring every vital function, even breathing for her. The doctors and nurses that attended to her were dressed head to toe in personal protective equipment. It seemed to take forever just to scrub and suit up to check on the young patient.

Her family could not see or be near Sissy in the PICU. The risk of exposure to the contagion was too high. As a result, and because of the trauma to a small child when there can be no family interaction, Sissy was kept heavily sedated.

Ryan stayed in the PICU's family waiting area, unable to see Sissy but not wanting to be around Anne or Danny for fear of infecting them. He had developed a cough but could not face the fact that he might have the virus. Anne booked a hotel room at the Holiday Inn near the medical center for herself and Danny. The CDC had asked them to quarantine there for at least ten days, limiting outside contact to visits with Sissy's doctors at the medical center, and arranging food supplies. She and Ryan kept in contact by phone and Danny stayed busy with cable TV and computer games on his dad's laptop.

"Can you please tell me what is going on?" Anne pleaded with the doctors tending to Sissy. She could tell they were concerned, tired, and appeared to be stressed themselves given the long hours they were spending with Sissy and in counsel together.

Responding through plastic face shields and covered head to toe in personal protective equipment that looked more like space suits, their answers seemed cold and impersonal. "Mrs. Krause, I'm afraid we still don't have any answers. This is an unknown virus that is not responding to any of our treatments. We are working with the CDC hoping to have some answers soon."

"But how is my daughter?" Anne reached out to touch the doctor. She needed reassurance as well as answers.

The doctor pulled his arm back. "Let's avoid contact. I would have to scrub and change all over again. Because this is an unknown contagion, we don't know yet how it is spread. It is for your safety as well as others that we not touch." He then softened his voice in understanding. He was a father himself. He could imagine what she was going through. "Mrs. Krause, Sissy is in very serious condition. The virus is attacking her lungs. I'm afraid if we do not find an effective treatment soon, her condition could worsen; she could even die. I assure you, we are working around the clock doing everything we can to find a solution."

"Thank you." Anne wiped the tears from her cheeks.

Two days later, Ryan began running a fever in addition to his cough.

"Mrs. Krause," a hospital administrator met with Anne and Danny. He wore a face mask, disposable gown, and latex gloves. "I'm afraid your husband has tested positive for the virus and we have now admitted him. We have some paperwork we need for you to fill out. We will need to keep your husband in isolation for ten days. We understand you have not had any contact with him since leaving the ship?"

Anne nodded.

"Provided that his symptoms do not worsen, you may still maintain contact by phone." He smiled and handed her two face masks. "We do not advise it, but if for some reason you and your son need to be here to meet with a doctor, we ask that you wear these."

Anne sat in shock, unable to speak.

"You and your son have been staying in self-quarantine in your hotel, correct?" He gestured for them to put on the masks.

Anne nodded and did as she was instructed, then helped Danny put on his mask.

"And how long has that been?" He looked at his clipboard.

"Five days."

"Um hm," the administrator nodded. "Well, if you or your son do not develop symptoms over the course of five more days, Mrs. Krause, the two of you could return to your home in . . . where do you live?"

"Atlanta," Danny quickly answered. "Atlanta, Georgia."

"Oh, that is far. Well, you and your mom could return to your home in Atlanta." He smiled again.

"Without my dad and sister?" Danny asked.

"That's right. You must be missing a lot of school."

"I don't mind. Well, how much longer are you going to keep them here?"

"For your father, as I said, at least ten days. For your sister?" he shook his head and stood to leave. "We don't really know." Turning to Anne he added, "I'll let you know if we need anything else, Mrs. Krause."

Anne thanked the administrator and she and Danny walked outside to get some fresh air and to make some phone calls. It was a relief to take off the face masks. She did not know how medical personnel could wear those all day long. She wrapped them in a clean tissue and tucked them in a side pocket of her purse.

She dreaded calling Ryan's parents back in Georgia. They would hound her for answers that she just did not have. And then they would probably want to fly to LA. To what? Sit in a hotel room in quarantine like she and Danny?

And what was Anne going to do at the end of their quarantine? She should definitely send Danny back to Atlanta. He had school. But she could not leave Sissy and Ryan in Los Angeles—especially not knowing . . . she could not even think about any outcome other than them both getting well. Somehow, she needed to stay positive that things would work out.

She needed to hear a sympathetic voice. Someone who really understood what she was going through. Taking out her phone and the address card, she keyed in the number for Salma.

"Anne, it's so good to hear your voice! How is Sissy?"

"About the same. The doctors say they keep trying new treatments, but nothing works. And now Ryan has been hospitalized with the virus." She took a deep breath to control her emotions.

"Anne, you be strong. Everything is going to be fine. I just know it."

"Thank you, Salma. How's your family doing?"

"Well, we're back home in Chicago. We held a small memorial service for grandmother after church on Sunday. A funeral could not be held because the CDC would not release her body just yet. They said they still have more tests to run; and most likely, all of the bodies from the virus will have to be cremated."

"I've never heard of such a thing." Anne sat down on a bench outside the medical center. Danny did cartwheels in the grass. The warm sun felt good after spending so much time inside the hotel room.

"I know," Salma responded. "We keep watching the news and asking the CDC questions, but we're not getting many answers."

"Well, I can tell you, from what I see in this hospital and from what the news is saying about other hospitals around here, they are filling up fast with people sick with this virus. And not just people from the cruise ship. Apparently, it's extremely contagious. We were told to stay in quarantine at the hotel. And today at the hospital, they gave us face masks to wear."

"The CDC asked us to stay home and avoid large crowds. It's all so strange. I thought this was some kind of flu, but it's lookin' more like a plague or something."

"The doctors here say it's an unknown virus; and until they know how it's transmitted, we have to be very cautious."

"That makes sense. You know there was a cruise ship in Miami a day or two after ours that had people with the same symptoms?"

"I heard that on the news. Thank goodness the media are following this story closely. They say the CDC is continuing to check on the passengers from both ships because the number of new people getting sick is growing exponentially every day. And, apparently cases are starting to show up in other areas of the country that they hadn't even anticipated."

* * *

Brandon and Aubrey Williams returned from their cruise through the Panama Canal on the *Antavia* eager to share their experience with family and friends. They arrived in Los Angeles, then flew home to Cleveland after a long layover in Denver. They had been screened by the CDC when the ship docked in LA, and they had been asked to avoid contact with others while traveling, and to self-quarantine at home for ten days once they returned home. Just as a precaution.

"We don't have any symptoms. This is crazy," Aubrey chatted with her neighbor. "We just want to get together with a few friends."

"Well, we can't wait to see your pictures. I've never been to the Panama Canal."

"So, we're having a party tomorrow night. The whole neighborhood is invited. Great food and drinks. We'll put the canal pictures up on the big screen. It'll be great!"

Over the next eight days, Aubrey and ten of her neighbors became sick with symptoms of the Panama Contagion.

Chapter 23

CIA BIOCHEMICAL LABORATORY
LANGLEY, VIRGINIA
OCTOBER 30

Edward Sipkema returned to Langley with the extracted samples from the Net's laboratory in Thailand.

"That was a quick trip," fellow lab associate Samuel Eikner said when Sipkema entered the CIA's biochemical laboratory. "Whatcha got?" He rubbed his gloved hands together and smiled like a kid about to dive into his favorite bowl of ice cream.

Donned in a Tyvek protective suit, gloves, and plastic face shield, and eager to start the analysis, Sipkema set the black briefcase on the lab table.

"Some scary stuff, I'm afraid." He opened the briefcase.

"Really? Like what?" Eikner peered inside at the coded vials.

"Like many of the deadliest known substances known to man, and probably a few that we've never seen before." Sipkema let out a deep breath of air at the amount of work he and his team had before them.

Eikner's eyebrow raised in serious interest. "This is going to take quite a while to test, identify, and label all twenty of these samples."

"You got that right."

"Good news, though," Eikner's voice lightened as he handed Sipkema a case report printout. "While you were gone, we did verify the CDC's identification of that new virus—the one they labeled PanCo. It is a more potent variation, but of the same strain as the Hainan coronavirus."

"That will help," Sipkema replied and patted Eikner on the back. "Because the first thing we have to do with these samples, is locate the antigen to that Panama Contagion."

"Are you sure it's in here?" Eikner looked again at the coded vials.

Sipkema shook his head. "No. But given all the sick people who got off those two cruise ships, and the people they've unknowingly infected since, we've got to hope and pray that it is. So, suit up because I expect we'll be working around the clock until we find it." Holding up several vials he added, "Let's start with these."

"There go my dinner plans," Eikner laughed. "I'll get the team together."

Chapter 24

"Target is approaching," Paramilitary Ops commander and rappel master Theo Walker whispered into his helmet's throat mic. He watched the lights of the cruise ship *Antavia* against the darkened sky through night vision binoculars, crouched on a steel beam on the underside of the Bridge of the Americas—the gateway to the entrance of the Panama Canal. The humid salty mist of the Pacific Ocean mixed with dirt and bird droppings left a slippery sludge everywhere. Vehicles rumbled overhead on the bridge's road surface, echoing within the massive steel structure, but caused no distortion in Walker's mic or distraction to his laser-sharp focus.

"Teams prepare to insert," Walker commanded.

Three ops teams crouched with Walker at various locations within the bridge's under-beams and listened to his instructions through ear buds inside their night vision helmets. These were not uniformed military forces. These experts wore plain black. Nor were these guerilla mercenaries recruited in back alleys. These forces were well educated—most with advanced degrees—and highly skilled, considered the most elite of the US special missions paramilitary force.

"Air Ops acknowledge," Theo Walker commanded into his mic.

"Roger."

"Standby. If target does not begin turn-around maneuver before reaching San Juan Hill, fire air-to-surface missiles until target is destroyed."

"Understood."

"All Ops," Walker continued, "if operations go as planned, we will remove target to a safe area outside the harbor and assess explosives onboard. If they are deemed unsafe to dismantle, target will be taken out to sea and destroyed." He then commanded, "Sea Ops, acknowledge."

"Roger."

"Standby for sea coordinates. We may need a ride back."

"Understood."

"Ground Ops, recover bridge gear then proceed to assigned locations."

"Roger that."

They waited.

Walker ordered, "Ready. All teams drop to 30 feet and hold for the Go."

The teams started their rapid rappel as the cruise ship began to move slowly beneath them, passing under the Bridge of the Americas heading for the canal's entrance. Each member had been strategically positioned at a spot under the bridge to land in an area on the ship necessary to quickly take control and carry out their mission.

"Go!" Walker barked.

Team 1 dropped first at the closest point of the ship's bow on its highest deck. Upon landing and detaching from their retracting ropes, they split up and proceeded down both sides of the ship. With weapons drawn, they descended down the staircases marked "Crew only." These passages would take them down the fifteen decks to the central corridor of the ship (referred to as the I-95). Because the ship's manifest listed a skeleton crew, the risk of running into someone was low. Nevertheless, the team members each carried a modified Honey Badger low visibility carbine assault rifle.

"On your right!" Team 1's leader captain Jake Davis yelled. Three enemy crewmen walking along the corridor were caught off-guard as members of Team 1 stepped off the bottom steps. Two of the crewmen dropped immediately as bullets cut through them. One darted behind a pillar.

Davis dealt with the third crewman while the rest of Team 1 spread out down the storage areas that ran along the I-95 corridor. As experts in all three categories of explosives—nuclear, mechanical, and chemical—since the type or types of explosives onboard were unknown, their job was to assess and deactivate all explosive devices. And, if possible, dismantle.

"Three enemy crew down," Davis radioed to Walker. "Assessment underway."

"Great," Walker replied.

Walker and the rest of Team 2 dropped to the ship immediately following Team 1 and proceeded down the bow stairs to deck 12 where the navigational bridge, or command center, ran the full width of the ship. This area operated twenty-four/seven, so it was always manned and highly secured. Team 2 needed to breach the center's security doors and take control of the ship.

Team 3 dropped midship and proceeded down to the lower aft area where the engine room was located. Led by naval engineer Stu "Cranny" Crandall, they stormed the engine room, anticipating one or two enemy crewmen. One mechanic was on duty, who was taken out without incident.

"Secure the area," Cranny ordered his team. They then began familiarizing themselves with the nuances of the diesel electric engines of the *Antavia.*

"Team 3 reporting," Cranny radioed to Walker. "One enemy crew down. Engine room secured. This baby's lookin' good."

"Got it," Walker replied.

Team 2 split up, going to each side entrance of the secured command center. Networks expert Jan Jenkins and Ops Commander Walker looped the security camera feeds above the doors while other team members used C4 with coordinated timer blasting caps to take out the locked doors on each side of the command center. Entering from both sides, they fired their rifles taking out everyone on the bridge, then spread out to the captain's quarters and other rooms taking out more crew for a total of ten. The ship's filed manifest had listed a barebones crew of sixteen. So, with the four already taken out, that left two enemy crewmen somewhere onboard the ship.

"Reverse engines!" Special agent and certified ship captain Brian Lindorff shouted.

Team members immediately began the process of stopping the ship's forward motion as it drew closer to San Juan Hill.

"Air Ops disengage! I repeat, disengage!" Walker ordered into his mic.

"Roger that," the Air Operations fighter pilot replied as he pulled up on his F-35 Lightning jet, engaging 40,000 pounds of thrust behind him. He would stay in the area in case they needed him to sink the ship at sea.

As Team 2 slowly brought the ship around, Team 1 continued their assessment of the explosives onboard.

"No nukes," Davis reported. "Most of the explosives are chemical. Very high powered and a lot of 'em. But stable. They knew what they were doing when they set these babies. These can be dismantled. Timers are being deactivated."

"Jan," Walker called to the networks expert who was now pushing keys at a console of computer screens, "what eyes do we have around the ship?"

Jan nodded as she quickly scrolled through the different camera feeds. "Besides the command center, . . . most decks, the engine area, down the I-95 corridor, and several in the crew's quarters."

"Any sign of our missing crewmen?"

She shook her head. "Screens are clear."

Walker acknowledged her reply then radioed all of his teams.

"All Ops standby," he instructed as he reviewed again the manifest's number of crewmen. "There are enemy still onboard with possible portable explosive devices. Locations unknown. So, we are heading out to sea. All teams secure your areas. Team 3 also secure fuel tanks. Air and Sea Ops standby for destination coordinates."

After a brief moment the navigator read off the coordinates in longitude and latitude.

Air and Sea Ops confirmed.

Walker continued, "Sea Ops, prepare for extraction of teams at destination."

"Roger."

"Air Ops, hold for instructions."

"So, you think there's a possibility those missing crew members have access to portable explosive devices?" the navigator asked Walker.

"I'd say it's a strong possibility. As a suicide crew, my guess is they've equipped themselves with explosive vests. We need to keep them away from the chemicals and fuel tanks downstairs. If we can do that, at most they might do some structural damage."

Walker then spoke into his throat mic. "Team 1, what part of the ship is over the most volatile chemicals?"

"That would be aft, sir. On the port side."

Walker tilted his head toward the door and ordered, "Jan, you and seven others secure that area for at least three decks above. More if you can. We need to stop these guys before they get near the lower decks." He then took over scanning the camera screens.

Jan nodded and her group headed out. They divided and moved down the stairways on both sides and in the center of the ship.

As Jan reached the port side on the exterior of deck 7, she saw one of the enemy crew wearing an explosives vest about a hundred feet in front of her. She crouched in the stairwell below the deck landing and fired her Honey Badger assault rifle, hitting him just before he started down the stairs to deck 6.

The vest exploded. The blast wind propelled her back down the stairwell shielding her from the full impact of the discharge. The explosion seemed to be echoing within the metal walls surrounding her. *Or is that ringing in the ears?* she thought, trying to take an assessment of her condition. It certainly was taking much longer than she wanted to suck air back into her lungs. Even having anticipated the blast thump to her chest, she could not compel her lungs to inhale. *A punctured lung?* Just then, her lungs filled with air and she let out a gasp. *Yeah, there's that C4 motor oil smell.* Except for the chest pressure and ringing in her ears, and probably a lot of bruises from hitting stairs in the fall, she concluded that she was no worse for wear and slowly got to her knees. As the debris settled and smoke began to clear, she crawled back up what was left of the stairs to survey the damage. The explosion took out three to four levels of decks in the aft port side of the ship—parts of decks 5, 6, 7, and part of deck 8; most of which looked to have been restaurants, shops, and lifeboat areas. All well above the waterline. No severe structural damage.

"What the hell was that?" Walker shouted into his mic.

In a hoarse whisper she replied, "One enemy with a vest on 7. I got him. He took out a good portion of 4 decks aft on the port side. Above the waterline."

"You okay?"

She coughed. "Sure. I'm going to have to find another way out of this area. There's a lot of heavy debris. I'll handle it."

"Keep me posted. Team 1, how are those chemicals?"

"Still stable."

"Sea Ops, how far out are you?"

"I have you in sight. Arrival two minutes."

"All teams prepare for extraction. Deck 4 starboard side. Two minutes," Walker ordered.

"What about the last enemy crewman?" someone asked.

"Keep an eye out, but it's a chance we'll have to take. The sooner we get off this boat the better. Move!"

Jan found herself trapped on the port side of the ship, opposite where the other team members would be extracting soon. She glanced at her watch. *Less than a minute.* She also noticed a deep gash in her left thigh. She was losing a lot of blood. *No time to deal with that.* Her heart pounded and her body ached, adding to the realization that she may not make it in time. Crawling through a small opening of a shattered wall in what appeared to have been a restaurant, Jan got to her feet and ran toward the kitchen area hoping to find clear passage to the lower decks and the other side of the ship.

The Sea Ops' forty-seven-foot Motor Lifeboat (MLB) powerboat pulled alongside the cruise ship's tender dock.

"Air Ops, standby," Walker ordered, eager to be off the *Antavia* and away from the explosives. "Teams extraction in process. Prepare for missile strike."

"Roger that." The F-35 Lightning fighter jet pilot brought his aircraft around and in line with the ship, preparing for missile launch.

All team members except Jan quickly boarded the powerboat.

"Jan, where are you?!" Walker barked from the powerboat.

No reply.

"Jan, do you copy?"

Moments passed.

"We can't wait," Walker shook his head.

The powerboat's pilot revved the engines in anticipation of a full throttle exit.

"Sir, I can go back in," Davis shouted above the engine noise.

"With enemy access to explosives? It's too risky!"

As the powerboat's engines whined in high idle awaiting Walker's command, Jan came running onto the dock—out of breath and covered in debris dust and ripped clothing, her left leg blood-soaked. She leapt into the powerboat.

"Let's move!" Walker shouted to the powerboat pilot who shoved the throttle forward.

"Glad you could join us," Walker high-fived Jan and smiled, genuinely relieved that all of his teams had made it. "Good job."

As soon as they sped far enough away, Walker issued the command, "Air Ops, destroy target!"

They then watched the night sky light up as missiles struck, triggering massive explosions that obliterated all but the smallest traces of the *Antavia*.

Chapter 25

CENTERS FOR DISEASE CONTROL (CDC)
ATLANTA, GEORGIA
NOVEMBER 4

Despite the president's request to hold off taking action, Dr. Gordon Sanderson at the CDC headquarters in Atlanta implemented pandemic protocols nationwide. CDC technicians set up screening stations at all major airports and passenger seaports and began checking all arriving travelers for fever and flu-like symptoms. Travelers were instructed to go home and self-quarantine for at least ten days. Hospitals began triage quarantining of patients exhibiting symptoms, and they required all medical personnel to take extra precautions in hand scrubbing before and after patient care, and in wearing new personal protective equipment for every patient.

I should have done this from the beginning, Dr. Sanderson thought. *I only hope it's not too late.*

The media and the public began raising questions as to why.

"Just precautionary measures," was the answer given.

That answer did not seem to fit with the actions being taken; but the seriousness of the situation, at least to the public, did not seem to be a concern. These were just flu-like symptoms. Something most people got a shot for every year, or they might get sick for a few days—no big deal. Those who were having adverse effects from this sickness were the elderly or young children with underlying health issues. No real cause for alarm, right?

The media wanted answers.

Why was the CDC making such a big deal about this virus? Wasn't it just the flu? Some naysayers were saying this was worse than SARS.

And why were people not just in the United States now but in other parts of the world becoming sick from this virus?

Where did it originate from?

Why don't doctors seem to know how to treat this? Was this the flu or not? Why was a coronavirus so different?

Don't we have a vaccine for this? If not, why don't we get one? How long will it take?

Why were some people wearing masks?

The CDC's laboratories ramped up their testing to learn more about the contagion. Until they could identify how it was being spread, they would not know how to stop the cycle of sickness. Was it transmitted through the air? Through touch? Through liquids? Then, they needed to find effective treatments for patients with the virus. Even the CDC's Emergency Operations Center, as the command center for public health threats throughout the world, began preparing tests and setting up protocols for a possible worldwide outbreak of the Panama Contagion.

But what the CDC or any place else in the world did not have was a vaccine, or any possibility of a vaccine. And coming up with one could take years to prepare.

"Dr. Sanderson, this is President Bradshaw calling. I thought we were going to hold off on upsetting the public about this virus thing." The president chuckled slightly, trying to keep his annoyance from showing in his voice.

"Mr. President," Dr. Sanderson spoke abruptly and with authority. He did not care if his annoyance showed. "I'm afraid upsetting the public is the least of your worries. Our labs have been working around the clock analyzing all of the samples from those two cruise ships, trying to pinpoint where and how this biochemical virus was introduced. Well, Mr. President, they narrowed it down to spray bottles on those cruise ships. That's right, spray bottles. This deadly manmade virus, for which we have no cure, no vaccine, no way of even slowing it down at this point, was sprayed onto the hands of the passengers. That means it quite possibly was a deliberate vicious attack."

Silence.

The president spoke almost in a whisper. "This was a terrorist attack?"

"Well, that's for your people to decide. But I can tell you, at the rate of new cases that we're seeing, until we know how this virus is transmitted so we can stop the cycle—let alone figure out how to treat it— this virus is going to spread like an out of control wildfire with not a drop of water in sight. I advise you to start taking this seriously now!"

"I understand. I'll take care of it."

Chapter 26

SHENZHEN, SOUTHERN CHINA
NOVEMBER 5

"Everything was carefully planned to the last detail," the Foreigner whined to his friend, Bao. They sat together in a darkened room in the back of one of Bao's massage parlors on the outskirts of Shenzhen. A hashish hookah sat on the floor between them, the charcoal embers providing a small glow of red light reflecting off a cloud of white smoke. The Foreigner had not slept in days fearing repercussions of the botched canal attack. He remembered well what was done to his brother for the failed Hainan conflict—he had been the one to carry out the death sentence.

"Ahh!" His hands pressed against the sides of his head. "How could it have gone so wrong?"

"This should have been your moment—your crowning achievement," Bao soothed and extended the hookah stem to Xavi to dull the pain.

He slowly inhaled then let the smoke out, filling the air round him with curling white vapor. "How could this happen?" he strained through gritted teeth.

"I know. I don't understand. You thought it all through." Bao was sympathetic. He knew firsthand what it felt like to have the best-laid plans come crashing down around him.

"The ship exploded out to sea. It never made it to the canal. Was it the demolitions crew? Did they screw up and the explosions went off too early?"

Bao shrugged and took another hit, only half-listening.

"Some thought the ship had been seen near the Bridge of the Americas—that it passed under then turned around. How could that be?" The Foreigner ran his hand through his hair. "Others say that it was another ship that returned to Panama City."

Bao began shaking his finger. "I blame your crew. They were not to be trusted. Someone must have paid them a higher price to blow the ship up at sea."

The Foreigner thought for a moment then shook his head. "No. There was more to it than that because the other explosions set to go off at various points around the canal area didn't go off either. The explosives were removed at every site. No. Somebody knew where those sites were. They had to have a map."

"Who could have known?"

The Foreigner leaned back against the wall. That was the question. He had been racking his brain for days trying to think of someone. Anyone.

He shook his head. Nothing was coming to mind. Then his eyes widened.

"There was this one guy at the shipping facility. A new guy in communications. I received a tip that he was blabbing about the Panama job. I went there to shut him up, but he had already shipped out. At least that's what Kamon said. She said he was a tall good-looking Chinese guy. In port a couple of days. Went drinking with a few of the guys. But he wasn't in the system and no one else I talked to had ever even heard of this Yi guy."

"Yi! The guy's name was Yi?" All of the air sucked out of Bao upon hearing the name he loathed.

"Yeah, that was it."

"A tall Chinese guy?" Bao gulped.

"That's what she said. I never saw him." Xavi looked confused.

Bao began laughing—so hard it sounded like a wheezing snort. Xavi wanted to hit him.

He sat up. "This isn't funny, Bao!"

"Oh, man. I don't believe it!" Bao sniveled and gasped as he tried to regain his composure.

Once he did and after taking a few deep breaths, he explained. "Yi is not in communications. And he certainly doesn't work on any ship owned by the Net."

"You know this guy?"

"Oh, yes," Bao nodded. "And so did your brother. Now I know exactly what happened. The same thing that happened at Hainan. And let me tell you, Yi is exactly who's responsible."

By the time Bao finished telling the Foreigner all about the events leading up to the Hainan conflict, Yi and Sarah's involvement, and the destruction of the Net's communications center in Wild Boar Island, Xavi was seething. There was not a punishment cruel enough that he could inflict upon Yi.

"But why would a Guangzhou judge want to destroy the Net?"

"That's what we would all like to know," Bao replied. "My friend, Tan Yang, suspects that Yi is a spy with the World Trade Organization. He tried to get the information out of Sarah. His attack put her in the hospital, but I don't think he got anything out of her."

"I need to speak with Tan Yang!" the Foreigner shouted. "Get him on the phone. Now!"

"Okay. Calm down."

"Don't tell me to calm down! I need to find out what he knows."

Bao keyed in Tan Yang's phone number. It rang numerous times but there was no answer. "This time of night? That's very strange. Something's wrong. I'll call a mutual friend."

He keyed in another number.

"This is Bao. . . . Yes, I know it's late. I'm trying to reach Tan Yang but he's not answering. . . . "

After a long pause Bao hung up his phone. He was white as a sheet.

"What's wrong? Where's Tan Yang?"

"Apparently he's dead. He fell from Yi's apartment balcony."

They both sat silent, analyzing this piece of information.

The Foreigner spoke first. "Do you think Tan Yang told him about the Net's plans?"

"Tan Yang didn't know anything, or care. He's been too busy hiding from authorities."

"Well, who else would have known? Somebody tipped this Yi guy off. Or at least sent him to our shipping facility. I know he was nosing around there."

Bao thought back to the events leading up to the Hainan conflict, the people involved, those who had been at Yalong Bay days before Bao's world came crashing down.

Who was at the resort besides Yi and Sarah?

There had been a lot of Americans from the embassy there. Could Yi have been connected to them?

Then it hit him. Like a bolt of lightning going off in his head. Why hadn't he thought of it before? Could the two men he hated most in the world actually have gotten together at Yalong Bay? They were there at the same time.

"I need to make another phone call."

He punched in the numbers and waited. After a few moments someone answered. Loud noise like music or a party could be heard in the background. He had called an old acquaintance—a doorman—at the casino of his business partner João Araújo.

"This is Bao. By chance, has anyone by the name of Yi been to the casino recently to see Araújo?"

Bao waited, then nodded. A smile crossed his lips as he hung up the phone. He began gayly applauding himself and smiling his smirky smile.

"Yes, just as I thought!" he squealed. "Yi paid a visit to our dear friend Mr. Araújo last month and left carrying one of the Net's hard hats." Bao could not get the words out fast enough. He was beside himself with glee because he finally felt vindicated for the Hainan conflict. At last he could move on with his life. And, if he played his cards right, the Foreigner would take care of Yi and his business partner, Mr. João Araújo, once and for all.

"I have solved it for you!" he howled and continued lightly clapping.

The Foreigner held up his hand for Bao to be quiet. He needed to think. His eyes narrowed as he thought through his plans.

He calmly took out his phone and keyed in the number of Kamon's office. It was late so he would just leave her a message. And she would not be expecting him tomorrow, but he would be there—he had some important items to pick up.

"Kamon, schedule a meeting for me with Mr. João Araújo in his Macau office."

Chapter 27

MACAU, SOUTHERN CHINA
NOVEMBER 6

The Foreigner arrived at Macau international airport just after one o'clock in the afternoon. His meeting with Mr. Araújo was scheduled for 2:30. Since this was a business meeting, the Foreigner wore an Italian wool and silk navy pinstriped suit with a burgundy silk tie. He carried his small black case.

He extended his business card to the doorman at the casino and said, "I have a 2:30 appointment with Mr. Araújo."

The doorman nodded and placed the call.

He then opened the door and instructed the Foreigner to step inside.

"I will need to run this metal detector over your body," the doorman stated, pointing to the security wand in his right hand.

"Okay. Is there a problem?" The Foreigner set down his black case and held his arms out to the side.

"Just procedure."

The doorman ran the wand around him. It beeped at his right pants pocket.

"Would you mind emptying your pocket?" He held out a small basket.

"No problem." In it he placed keys, some change, and his switchblade knife. "I will get that back?"

"On your way out."

When they arrived at Mr. Araújo's office door, the doorman knocked, then opened it enough to put his head in and said, "All clear."

Araújo replied, "Let him in."

Mr. Araújo stood but remained behind his desk. He gestured for the Foreigner to sit in one of the chairs opposite his desk.

The Foreigner nodded and smiled, then took a seat.

The doorman closed the door and left.

"To what do I owe this pleasure?" Araújo spoke first. A slight tension lingered in his words.

The Foreigner waved his hand in the air. "Mostly pleasure. Maybe some business. We haven't had a chance to meet yet. I thought it was time." He smiled.

"That's fine. . . . And your brother? How is he?"

The Foreigner had not expected that question and squirmed a little. "He has not been around for some time."

"On vacation?" Araújo persisted.

"An accident. . . . I'm afraid he died."

"Oh, dear. I am sorry to hear that. I considered him a good friend." Araújo took out a cigarette and lit it. He did not offer one to his guest. "Well, what is it that I can do for you today?"

The Foreigner leaned back in the chair and let out a deep breath. "I wonder if you could tell me about a gentleman by the name of Yi."

Araújo thought for a moment then nodded.

"Yes. He was here a month or so ago. Concerned about some shipping violations on Net vessels in Guangzhou. I referred him to your facility in Thailand. That's the last I saw of him."

The Foreigner nodded.

"And how do you know this Yi person?"

"Well, it's funny really. We met on a bus heading to the Sanya airport after staying at the Yalong Bay resort in Hainan. He commented on my watch and we exchanged pleasantries and business cards. We were scheduled to be on the same flight back to Guangzhou then we both changed to the same alternate flight. I didn't see him again until last month, which reminded me of that first flight we were supposed to be on—the one that your guy took to the bottom of the South China Sea. And by the way, I don't appreciate someone from your organization attempting to take my life!"

"That wasn't the Net's doing. That was Bao."

Araújo nodded. "I assumed so."

"So, who is this Yi character?"

Araújo took out Yi's business card and handed it to the Foreigner.

That is all I know about him. He said he was a judge in the Guangzhou administrative courts."

"Bao thinks there's more to him than that."

Araújo let out a puff of smoke. "Bao thinks a lot of wrong things."

"So does Tan Yang. And now Tan Yang's dead."

"Tan Yang's dead? I'm sorry to hear that. How did he die?"

"He fell from Yi's balcony, that's how. Or he was pushed. Apparently Tan Yang beat up his girlfriend—a judge named Sarah—who he tried to get information from because he thought Yi was a spy."

Araújo's eyebrows raised then he shook his head. "I don't know anything about that."

The Foreigner opened the black case and took out a small straw. He then stood up and walked over to Araújo's desk by the phone. He picked up the handset and handed it to Araújo.

Setting Yi's business card on the desk, he said, "I want you to call Yi and get him here. As soon as possible. Invite him to dinner tonight as your guest. Be very pleasant but tell him it's urgent." Then with a harsh sneer he added, "Just get him here!"

Araújo put out his cigarette and shook his head. "I don't think this kid is who you think he is."

The Foreigner blew through the straw directly at Araújo. A sticky substance landed on his cheek and nose. Araújo reached up and touched the gel with his fingers and looked at it then looked at the Foreigner. A curious look crossed his face.

"What is this?" he questioned, but terror began spreading through his mind. An answer could not come quick enough.

The Foreigner just smiled.

"Are you insane? You got this in my nose!" Panic set in as he tried to wipe it off but only spread it more as it quickly dissolved into his skin.

The Foreigner held up his hand. "Don't worry. I have the antidote. And I will administer it if you do as I ask." He smiled again.

"But what is this?" Araújo was afraid to even move.

The Foreigner let out a menacing chortle. He so enjoyed the drama. "Well, you probably don't really want to know. . . . But I will tell you anyway. It is a flesh-eating bacteria that in about ten hours will advance beyond the help of the antidote."

Araújo grabbed the phone and dialed Yi's number.

The Foreigner wiggled his finger back and forth with a smirk on his face. Of course, Araújo would not pull a fast one. His life was now on the line. The Foreigner then pointed his finger downward and pushed the speaker button on the phone. He wanted to hear the whole juicy conversation.

Araújo took a deep breath to calm his nerves. He needed to sound believable to pull this off.

"This is Yi."

"Yi, this is John Araújo."

"Yes, John. It's nice to hear from you."

"Thank you. I hope you were able to resolve those shipping violations without any problem."

"None at all. Thank you again for your help."

Araújo cleared his throat then said, "I was hoping I could ask a favor in return. A rather urgent one. If you are available for dinner, I would like to invite you to my casino this evening, say six o'clock?"

"Well, John, I have an early court hearing I was hoping to prepare for this evening . . ."

Araújo interrupted, "Please, Yi, this is a very urgent matter. I wouldn't ask if it wasn't important."

"John, is everything okay? You sound . . . distraught."

The Foreigner gave Araújo a stern look.

Araújo took a breath to steady his nerves. "No, No! Everything is fine. I'm sorry if I have alarmed you. It's just that time is of the essence on this. I really need your help this evening."

Yi thought for a moment. "Okay, John, if it's that important. I'll be there at six."

"Great. I'll meet you at my office."

They both disconnected the call.

Araújo sat back in his chair and let out a nervous sigh of relief. Beads of perspiration began forming on his forehead and neck.

"Okay, Xavi, let's have the antidote."

"Not until Yi is here in this room."

Maybe it was his imagination, but he could already feel a burning in his nostrils.

"Please, Xavi!"

"We have time. Oh, and I'll take whatever guns you keep in this office."

Araújo opened a side drawer of his desk and handed him his 9mm automatic.

* * *

The Foreigner enjoyed several drinks from the well-stocked liquor cabinet to pass the time while Araújo chain-smoked for over two hours. Red blotches had spread across his fingers and hands and black centers had begun to form in the red areas on his face and neck. He could no longer feel his nose and his lungs were feeling congested. He assumed that was from the continual cigarette smoke.

The phone rang at 5:50. It was one of the doormen. Yi had arrived.

The Foreigner opened his black case and prepared a syringe.

"Is that the antidote?" Araújo was shaking in anticipation of finally getting some relief.

"Not yet. This is something I brought specially for Yi." He held the needle up and flicked it to remove any air bubbles. Not that an air embolism to the heart wouldn't be an exciting thing to watch.

"Have Yi sit in the chair when he comes in," the Foreigner instructed.

The doorman knocked.

"Come in!" Araújo eagerly shouted. "Please come in!"

Yi was startled when he saw Araújo.

"John, are you alright?"

Araújo took Yi by the arm and led him to the chair.

"I'll be fine, Yi. Please, just sit down. I'll be fine." The beads of perspiration were now running down Araújo's face.

Yi noticed the man standing off to the side. He looked vaguely familiar.

As Araújo started to say something else, the Foreigner stepped behind Yi and plunged the syringe into his neck.

Yi's quick reflexes knocked the syringe from the Foreigner's hand and he bolted from the chair, but not before a lethal amount of the contagion had entered his body.

"I'm so sorry, Yi. I had no choice," Araújo cried. Overcome with guilt, and weakened by the bacteria now destroying his body, he collapsed to his knees on the floor.

His hands clasped in front of him, he begged. "Please, Xavi, give me the antidote now."

"So you're Xavi." Yi didn't know whether to take Xavi out or try to help Araújo.

Looking at Araújo, the Foreigner replied, "Oh, I'm afraid I left that in my other case." He covered his mouth as if stifling a chuckle.

Araújo's body collapsed to the floor. Yi dashed to the phone and called for help.

"It's too late," the Foreigner said casually as he closed his black case. "He has a flesh-eating bacteria. And as for you, that injection was a little virus I brought back from Panama. Such a high concentration will begin to take effect in a matter of hours rather than days." He pulled out the gun and moved toward the door.

Ignoring the Foreigner, Yi checked Araújo for a pulse and began chest compressions. Maybe there was a chance to save him. He had to at least try.

Both doormen came into the office and ran toward Araújo. The Foreigner stepped into the doorway.

"And now, gentlemen, I will exit this establishment without any incident, or many other people will die. Understood?"

"An ambulance is on its way," one of the doormen said to Yi. He nodded and continued the compressions. Glancing toward the door, he saw that the Foreigner was gone.

The ambulance arrived within ten minutes, but João Araújo was pronounced dead.

When Yi left the casino, his head was spinning. Not from the injection, but from the loss of João Araújo. He liked him. João had been one of the few people outside of this assignment that Yi had actually enjoyed. Now, all he felt was . . . he wasn't even sure. He just felt numb.

As he walked back to the train station, he thought about his assignment as a judge in Guangzhou, his first day there when he learned about the murdered tax assessor, then Tan Yang and his corrupt activities and his connections with Bao. Bao—the man he almost killed with his own hands. Could he have really done that? He thought back to the Hainan Conflict when Bao attacked him on the beach. He held Bao's neck in his bare hands, and he wanted to squeeze. It would have been so easy. But he believed in the rule of law. It was not his right to take matters into his own hands. But what happened? Bao escaped. He was a free man. And now more people had died. And then there was the Foreigner. Clearly a psychopath. Were there more like him in this Net organization? Yi knew what he was feeling. A cold hardness was starting to form inside him. He did not want it to, but it was growing there nonetheless. And he could not stop it.

* * *

Something else was not sitting well with Yi. Symptoms rapidly began appearing. Cough, fever, nausea, tightness in his chest. By the time the train arrived back at the Guangzhou train station, he knew he was going to be sick. Very sick. *Xavi had said the virus would take effect within hours.* Yi thought he would have time to get back to his apartment. *I just need my American ID.* As the train doors opened, he exited in time to vomit in the bushes.

Yi sat down on one of the platform benches. A lightheadedness washed over his mind like a milky cloud and the tightness in his chest made it difficult to breathe. He took out his cell phone and Edward Sipkema's business card from his suit pocket. The business card was plain white—no logo—with his name, PhD Microbiologist, and a phone number. Yi quickly keyed in the number.

Ed answered on the second ring.

"Sipkema."

"Ed, this is Yi. In Guangzhou. I need help." Breathing was becoming more difficult. Yi pulled at his tie and collar. "The Net injected me with a high concentration of the contagion."

"Yi, exactly where are you?"

He was now so weak he could barely get the words out. "Guangzhou train station. . . . East side . . . platform . . . by the payphone. . . . Can't . . . brea. . ."

"Yi?"

No response.

Yi slumped over on the bench. He tried to conserve oxygen as his lungs refused to take in air and darkness began to surround him. This time there were no stars, only blackness.

Edward quickly dialed the number of a hospital near the train station and, in perfect Cantonese, ordered an ambulance to locate Yi at the east platform by the payphone, give immediate medical assistance, and treat as contagious. He then called the US Consulate in Guangzhou.

"Agent Cheryl Timmons, please," he directed the operator. After a short pause she answered.

"This is Agent Timmons."

"Cheryl, Ed Sipkema here. We need to extract a NOC agent enroute to the Guangzhou East Medical Center. He has been injected with a deadly virus for which, at this point, only Langley has an antigen. He's got to be quarantined right away—this is nasty stuff. I need you to get one of our medical teams over to the hospital right away, get him quarantined and on a respirator if needed, and then get him onto a medical transport to Langley as soon as you can. I'm afraid his life is going to depend on it."

"What's the agent's name?"

"Yi. He's assigned to Guangzhou as an administrative judge."

Agent Timmons keyed the information into her database. After scanning through numerous entries, she located him.

"Jichun or Jason Yi. I found him. And he's headed to Guangzhou East Medical Center?"

"By ambulance. That's correct."

"I'll take it from here. Thanks Ed."

"I owe you one, Cheryl."

Cheryl smiled at the number of times she had heard that phrase. It was all part of the job, and she loved it.

First, she needed to arrange a medical team from the State Department to take over Yi's medical care and handle the quarantine. She would arrange that by phone. Then, she needed to schedule the flight back to Langley. She would not rest until those two things were done. Then she could start the paperwork of canceling his job, apartment, utilities, and arranging for his things to be packed up and sent back to the States.

Agent Jason Yi, you are going home.

Chapter 28

The chartered medical flight arrived at Reagan National Airport in Washington, DC. Yi's mobile quarantine unit and the medical team treating him were then transferred by helicopter to Sibley Memorial Hospital. Edward Sipkema waited with a syringe of what the CIA believed was the antigen to the Panama Contagion. But first, Edward needed a sample of Yi's blood to verify that the virus he carried matched the pathogen they had. If the viruses did not match, this antigen would not help and could actually hurt him.

Yi floated in and out of consciousness during the flight. Several times his deceased grandfather visited him, and Yi wondered if he had died and passed to the other side. But since other deceased ancestors had not come to meet him, it all seemed so confusing. His grandfather wore his usual leather cap and cotton rain jacket, and he walked slightly stooped with his hands clasped behind his back. They walked together along a peaceful river path and talked about Guangzhou and Yi's work.

"Have I died, *yeye?*"

"It is not your time, *suner.* You have done a great work. But there is more to be done."

Those words repeated over and over in Yi's mind. *There is more to be done.* He wanted to do more, but for some reason he could not move. There was a powerful nothingness holding him in place.

"I'm very skeptical about this," Sibley Memorial's infectious diseases specialist Dr. Khatri said to Edward as they transferred Yi's quarantine unit into an isolation room in the hospital's Intensive Care Unit. "This antigen is an unknown; therefore, a very high risk. We need more time to run some tests."

"We've matched this antigen to the pathogen in his blood. It's all we've got," Edward replied, preparing the syringe.

As the quarantine transfer was completed and Yi was hooked up in Sibley Memorial's ICU, Dr. Khatri continued his discussion with Edward. "We don't know what effect this might have on his immune system. By giving this to him now, we could create antibody dependency and make matters even worse. Let's at least run a lab test. We must check our facts."

"Waiting for the results would take days. You know that. He doesn't have days. If we don't try something now, it's a fact he's going to die," Edward glared.

"His lungs are already starting to shut down," one of the doctors from his chartered medical flight replied, a glint of hopelessness creeping into his eyes. He began to push the now empty quarantine unit out of the ICU for transport back to the airport. It had been a long flight from China. He was skeptical that Yi was going to make it. But they had done everything they could do. It was now in the hands of the CIA and the expert staff at Sibley Memorial.

Edward shook his head. "We have no choice." He prepared the skin site and injected the antigen into Yi's upper arm muscle.

"God help us," Dr. Khatri muttered as he and the other doctors watched Edward administer the unknown substance.

"Let's hope so," Edward completed the injection then nodded and stepped to the back of the group to watch the antigen's effect, even knowing that it might be days before they would see any change in Yi's condition.

Chapter 29

"This White House press briefing," Press Secretary Avery Wallace began, "is for release of the president's proclamation declaring a national emergency regarding the recent outbreak of the Panama Contagion, to keep the citizens of the United States well informed as quickly as possible, and to give notice of his signed executive order establishing policy and regulations for procedures pertaining to individuals exhibiting symptoms of the PanCo virus. President Bradshaw has acted swiftly and efficiently to address these concerns, and he has signed and issued this order based on guidelines set by the CDC and the World Health Organization.

"Over the course of the past three weeks, the United States and other parts of the world have seen a rapid increase in the number of cases of this virus. In the United States alone, over 27,000 cases have been documented so far with 4,000 deaths, rendering this outbreak a major pandemic.

"The President has directed the federal government to take the necessary steps to contain this virus; however, such actions will require the support of state, local, and even individual citizens to stem the tide of this contagion. The CDC's computer models indicate that the virus spike has not begun to peak as yet. Until this happens, the daily cases and death rate will continue to increase exponentially if these procedures are not followed.

"Individuals with symptoms are asked to self-quarantine in their homes for at least ten days. People are encouraged to work from home when possible. When in public, it is advised to social distance at least six feet apart and to wear face masks. Practice frequent hand washing with soap and water, and use hand sanitizer when available.

"States are asked to carefully monitor their hospitals' available resources, including ICUs, beds and ventilators, and to stockpile sufficient supplies for projected caseloads. Medical staff should be well protected with disposable personal protective equipment (PPEs) and staff should be monitored regularly for symptoms. Test kits are available through the government.

"Food and grocery supplies may come under short supply. There is to be no stockpiling of essential items, and no price gouging.

"Unessential businesses or businesses that cannot provide physical distancing of six feet are asked to close their doors until further notice.

"I will now open up this briefing for questions."

A sea of media hands shot into the air.

"Yes, the reporter in the front, what is your question?" Avery asked, pointing into the audience.

The reporter stood and asked, "Do we know how this contagion from Panama got started?"

"Yes," Avery replied. "According to the investigations by the CDC and the World Health Organization, "numerous tourists and crew members from the cruise ships went on a Panama jungle excursion and came in contact with the virus through animal secretions—possibly of the frog family. Because they then exposed others on the ships as well as in their travels home to states and other countries, we are now seeing this rapid increase of cases."

A flurry of cameras and recording devices clicked and flashed.

"Next?" she pointed out another reporter.

"What is the difference between this virus and the flu? What makes this virus worse?"

"It may not necessarily be worse. Some people may not experience severe symptoms. However, this virus—which is a coronavirus not influenza—can attack the cells lining the lungs. Therefore, if it progresses far enough, the lungs and other vital organs of the body can shut down, which ultimately may lead to death."

"When will there be a vaccine?"

"The president continues to work very hard on this matter and he believes a vaccine will be available very soon. That is all for now. Thank you."

Chapter 30

"Mrs. Krause, this is Dr. Gordon Sanderson from the CDC in Atlanta. I understand you have a daughter with the PanCo virus being cared for at Harbor-UCLA in Los Angeles."

"Yes, doctor, this is Anne Krause. That is correct. My daughter, Sissy, is at Harbor-UCLA."

"I hope you don't mind that the hospital gave me your contact information. I have been following your daughter's case quite closely. I believe I may have a possible treatment that, while there are no guarantees and it is not an approved treatment, I believe it may be effective in your daughter's case."

"Oh, doctor, that is wonderful news!"

"Well now, I don't want to get your hopes up. As I said, it is not approved. In fact, it has not yet been tested on humans. But it has been extremely effective in our lab tests, and the side effects would be minimal, if any. It will either help your daughter or have basically no effect. I felt it was at least worth mentioning to you."

"Thank you, doctor, I definitely want to hear more about it."

"Well, we have a gentleman in Washington, DC who was exposed to an extremely high dose of the Panama Contagion. As a result, his body is producing large quantities of antibodies that are fighting the virus in his body. His blood type happens to match your daughter's. I believe that by putting some of those antibodies from his blood plasma into your daughter, that her body would be better equipped to fight off this virus."

"That makes sense. Has this man recovered from the virus?"

"Not as yet. No."

Silence. Anne did not know how much more she could take. She would do anything to make Sissy well, but she did not think that included making her a guinea pig.

"What about my husband, Ryan?" she asked.

"If I received his medical records correctly, he is recovering from the virus and should be released shortly. He would not benefit from this treatment."

"What if he were the donor for our daughter?"

"Well, the principle would be the same; but the number of antibodies would be much lower. A lesser quantity may be of no value, I'm afraid."

"I see." Anne thought for a moment. "And with this other person's blood there would be no side effects?"

"No more so than with a blood transfusion."

"Uh hm." She tried to think of something else. Her brain was so tired. "May I discuss this with my husband Ryan and get right back with you?"

"Of course. You may call me at this number any time."

"Thank you, doctor." She paused, then asked, "Um, if we went ahead with this, how quickly would it happen?"

"I would be on a plane to Los Angeles within twenty-four hours."

"You would do this yourself?"

"With a team of specialists, yes."

"Thank you, Dr. Sanderson. You don't know how much this means to us. I will call you as soon as we decide. Bye."

She then called Ryan and after a brief discussion, they both felt it was the best thing to do. They had to try every possible treatment to save Sissy's life. Anne phoned Dr. Sanderson back with their decision.

Dr. Sanderson's team collected the blood plasma sample from Yi then flew to Los Angeles to administer the antibody treatment on Sissy. Within three days she started showing signs of improvement.

"Dr. Sanderson, I can't thank you enough," Anne said as she hugged the doctor with tears in her eyes. "You have saved our daughter's life."

The doctor smiled and shook his head. "No. We just administered the treatment. The man you have to thank is named Jason Yi, and it's a miracle he's alive." He then let out a deep sigh. It had been a long ordeal and he was tired. He felt partly to blame for not having implemented CDC protocols earlier. He certainly would not make that mistake again. "This all should never even have happened," he added, half under his breath.

"I know," Danny said as he walked up to the doctor. "I saw the bad guy spraying people on the ship. That's what made everybody sick, isn't it?"

Dr. Sanderson leaned over to face Danny and put his hands on his shoulders. "Yes," he nodded. "How did you know that?" He then looked up at Ryan and Anne. "Our labs traced the source of the virus to spray bottles onboard the ship."

Ryan put his hand on the back of Danny's head.

"Danny, do you know who the person was that was doing the spraying?"

Danny shook his head. "Jemila and I saw him. He was wearing officer Vikram Padilla's uniform, but it wasn't Vikram. We spoke with Vikram earlier. He was really nice."

"Do you have any idea who this other man was?" Dr. Sanderson asked. "What he looked like?"

"No," Danny shook his head. "But he had a handkerchief with an X on it. And he didn't know what Oscar meant."

Dr. Sanderson looked puzzled. "Oscar?"

"Yeah, it means Man Overboard. Anybody who works on a cruise ship would know that."

The doctor stood up. "Danny, you've been very helpful." He then shook Danny's hand.

After a week Sissy was taken off the ventilator and could breathe on her own. At ten days she was moved out of the PICU to a regular room and her family was allowed to visit her wearing facial masks to avoid re-infecting her, since the doctors did not know how long the antibodies would keep her immune. They expected that, with home quarantining and close monitoring, she would be able to go home within another week.

It would still be months if not a year before a vaccine could be developed from the small amount of antigen the CIA had extracted from the Net's Thailand facility; then have it FDA-tested, approved, and mass-produced sufficient for the world. But at least the treatment of blood plasma antibodies donated from recovering virus patients had proven to be an effective short-term treatment for seriously ill patients with the Panama Contagion.

Chapter 31

SIBLEY MEMORIAL HOSPITAL
WASHINGTON, DC
NOVEMBER 30

On the morning of November 30th, the nurses noticed signs that Yi was coming out of his coma. His vitals had returned to normal, he was breathing on his own, they had observed muscle movement in his fingers and twitching in his eyelids. He had been moved out of ICU into a large private room. Sarah had been by his bedside since the Thanksgiving holiday break, and now others had gathered in his room as well. Dr. Khatri, Edward, Senator Boyle, Mark Stanton, and even Dr. Sanderson stood in his hospital room in anticipation of him waking up.

"Yi, can you hear me?" Sarah whispered to him through her face mask as she leaned close to his ear. She held his right hand in her hands.

"If you can hear me, squeeze my hand."

She felt a slight movement in his fingers.

"Try again," Dr. Khatri said.

"See if you can squeeze my hand, Yi," Sarah said, a little louder this time.

Yi squeezed her hand.

"Yes!" Others in the room chimed in together.

"He's coming out of it," Dr. Khatri said as he walked over to Yi's bedside and leaned over to look at his eyes. "Yi, can you open your eyes?"

Slowly, Yi began to open his eyes. The lights were so bright, he quickly closed them again.

"Dim the lights," Dr. Khatri instructed, pointing to the wall.

Edward walked over and turned off half the room's lights.

"Try again, Yi," Dr. Khatri, said.

Yi blinked his eyes, then slowly opened them. He glanced around the room. People were dressed head to toe in white. Caps, gowns, face coverings, gloves, and booties. He blinked again, confused, then asked, "Is this heaven?"

Mark Stanton stepped forward and stated, "Jason, this is Director Stanton . . ."

"Oh," Yi moaned and shut his eyes, "this must be hell."

Everyone burst out laughing.

When it quieted back down, Sarah spoke. "Yi, this is Sarah. You're in the hospital. I'm here with you. You're going to be okay."

"Sarah? No! You shouldn't be here!" Yi thrashed from side to side.

Sarah burst into tears and ran from the room.

Edward moved to Yi's side. "Yi, this is Edward. You called me, remember? You were injected with the virus. I brought you here to the States to administer the antigen. You're in Washington, DC now."

Yi slowly opened his eyes and began to focus on Edward.

"Oh, man, Edward. I thought I was still in China. Would you go get Sarah? Please," he added with urgency.

"Sure, Yi." Edward quickly left to find her.

Yi took a deep breath. His strength was gone. He was so confused. He really thought he had died in China.

He blinked a few times to clear his vision then looked around the room. It was not his imagination. There really were other people in the room dressed in white.

"Did I hear correctly that Director Stanton was here?" Yi asked.

"Yes, Jason, I'm here." Director Stanton stepped forward.

"Director, I must thank you and all of the people involved in bringing me here and saving my life. Especially Edward. I can't believe how quickly this all happened. I owe him my life."

"Don't worry about that, Jason. You job is to get well."

A brief pause.

"I would like to introduce myself," Dr. Sanderson said as he stepped forward. "I am Dr. Gordon Sanderson, Deputy Director of Infectious Diseases at the CDC in Atlanta, Georgia."

Yi slowly extended his hand. "It's a pleasure."

"No, the pleasure is mine," the doctor said as he lightly squeezed Yi's hand.

"First off," he then added with an awkward chuckle, "I don't know if I should address you as Jason or Yi—I've heard both."

A slight smile touched the corners of Yi's mouth. "Please call me Yi."

"Yi it is. Yi, I wanted to personally thank you for being the instrument for saving literally thousands of lives."

"What?" Yi was not sure he had heard correctly.

"That's right. Your blood plasma, because of its high content of antibodies to this virus and because your AB blood type is the universal donor for plasma, allowed us to successfully test and thereby establish an effective antibody treatment for this virus. Until we have a vaccine, it is all we've got. And we couldn't have done it without you."

"Well, I wouldn't want to do it again, but I'm glad I could help."

"I don't know how you came to have such a high dose, but we now know this virus was introduced onboard two cruise ships by way of spray bottles, sprayed onto passengers' hands. We don't know anything about the man, but one of the persons spraying the virus had a handkerchief with the letter *X* on it."

"I know exactly who that was," Yi responded. "His name is Xavi. He's known as the Foreigner and he works for the Net organization."

"We suspected as much," Stanton responded.

"Is that who injected you?" Edward asked.

Yi nodded then quickly added, "Edward, you're back! Did you find Sarah? Is she here?"

"I'm here," Sarah replied, a little hesitantly.

"Sarah, I'm so sorry! Please, come here."

She moved to the chair she had been sitting on.

"I'm sorry, but could I have a moment alone with Sarah? Please?"

"Oh, sure," everyone said in unison as they stepped outside the room.

"First of all," Yi said very tenderly to Sarah, "please take off that mask."

"That's very risky, Yi. Not for me but if you were to become infected again it could be fatal."

"That's a risk I will take."

Sarah took down the mask. Yi smiled then gently pulled Sarah close for a passionate kiss.

"I'm sorry for making you feel unwanted, Sarah. But I genuinely thought I was still in China and that you had come there. It's not safe for you. Now more than ever."

"I know, Yi. I understand."

"No, you don't," Yi shook his head. "It's not just Bao anymore. I'm afraid the Foreigner may target you as well. The guy is crazy. I've seen what he can do." Yi became agitated.

Sarah placed her hands upon Yi's chest to calm him. "Why would he target me? This new Foreigner doesn't even know me."

Yi hesitated. He knew Sarah was not going to react well. "Because I killed Tan Yang."

"You did what?!" A look of horror crossed her face.

"It was an accident, Sarah. He fell from my balcony after we fought. It was an accident."

Director Stanton stuck his head back in the room. "Is everything okay in here? Can we come back in? There are things we need to discuss." He seemed a little impatient, as usual.

"Just one more minute, Director," Yi replied.

The director nodded, held up his hands in acknowledgment then left the room.

Yi looked deep into Sarah's eyes. He could see uneasiness there. "We'll work this out, Sarah. And as long as you are here in the States, you'll be safe. I'll see to it." He pulled her close again and kissed her.

She smiled, but in her heart the uneasiness grew.

Sarah gestured for the others to re-enter the room.

Dr. Sanderson spoke first. "If I may say one more thing, I'll then be on my way. I understand from Director Stanton that Yi and Edward are responsible for acquiring this antigen that has saved Yi's life. I will be taking some back to the CDC for further testing and formulation into a vaccine. We will then be able to move forward with FDA approval and mass-production for the whole world. To both of you, and the CIA's efforts in bringing this about, the CDC is extremely grateful."

He then shook hands with everyone and left.

Director Stanton spoke next. "Dr. Khatri, what is Jason's—I'm sorry, Yi's—prognosis?"

Dr. Khatri cleared his throat and looked down at the floor as if the answer were written there. "It's hard to know for sure, and assuming he doesn't become re-infected with the virus, I would say now that he has come out of the coma, I believe, remarkably, he may make a full recovery." The doctor then looked at Yi and shook his head. It really had been a miracle.

The director grinned and patted the doctor on the back. "I was hoping you would say that."

Stanton then turned to Senator Boyle. "Martin, when Yi recovers, I want him working for the CIA. I need him fully trained and focused on uncovering as much information as he can about the Net organization. We have got to learn about their leaders, who controls their operations and from where. And then we've got to eliminate them. Not just their operations centers and tactical facilities, I mean their headquarters, their leaders, their think tank, their financial backers, their strategic planners. I have assigned Ed Sipkema here to work with Yi, and whoever and whatever else they need. We are done playing games, Martin. We are going after this Net organization."

"Well," Boyle began, "I would think Yi would want some say in this."

"As a matter of fact, I would, sir," Yi replied with a grin. "Which is why I'm glad you're here."

"He's been here with me off and on the past three days," Sarah interjected.

"Good, so you've both met," Yi responded.

"Yes," the senator nodded. "I've been learning all about her work in Tibetan-Sino relations."

"And what an important addition that would be to your staff," Yi postured, "especially if I leave my position for the CIA."

"But I would need to finish my law degree at Temple University, and arrange a permanent work visa," Sarah said, holding her breath not believing that such a job in the States could be possible.

The Senator thought for a moment then nodded. "I believe that can all be arranged."

"Oh, Yi!" Sarah exclaimed.

"Just as I had planned," Yi smiled and gave Sarah a wink.

Chapter 32

"Although the planned cruise ship explosion at the canal was thwarted, our introduction of the Panama Contagion has succeeded in bringing the United States and much of the world to its knees," the white-haired man crowed to the Net directors at their quarterly meeting.

All of the directors except one applauded loudly.

"You realize that the number of deaths from exposure to this contagion far exceeded anticipated numbers," the medical director stated. "The strain proved to be far more deadly than we were led to believe. Had governments not initiated quarantine efforts when they did, and the antivirus located to neutralize it, a significant portion of the world's population could have died." He raised his voice as he added, "Why, it's barbaric to have taken such a risk! We may never even know the full impact of such foolishness. I want to go on record as having been opposed to the release of this deadly virus without further study and full disclosure of its potency."

"Your objection is noted," the white-haired man replied with a wave of his hand as if dismissing the comment. "The contagion served its purpose."

He continued. "By diverting US attention from the Middle East, the Net has been able to secure crude oil markets and thereby finance and control its trading. I am sure each of you has already experienced significant personal gains as we have set up investor indexes and manipulated inflation to our benefit. In addition, your pockets have been well lined by the numerous priceless relics that have been confiscated and re-distributed at your direction. Furthermore, weapons of mass destruction and large quantities of plutonium have been secretly moved to undisclosed locations—no longer under the watchful eye of the West."

Several directors exchanged looks of concern.

One director spoke up, "Uh, I don't believe we have been given the locations of any plutonium storage. Or the details of maintaining such storage facilities. If I remember correctly, the organization's bylaws require full disclosure of all Net assets and their locations. For safety reasons, we certainly do not want plutonium to be mishandled; or worse, to get into the wrong hands."

"Yes, of course you'll receive disclosure," the white-haired man interrupted. He paused while he took out his handkerchief, satin-stitched with a letter *X,* and wiped his brow. He seemed flustered and momentarily confused. After putting the folded cloth back in his pocket, he added in a derisive tone, "Now, may I please continue?"

The directors sat in silence, but the level of concern from at least three directors was increasing. The flustered behavior of their senior director was unusual; yet had manifested on several recent occasions.

"In addition, we have instigated genocide in two major countries and, as a result, inserted puppet leadership into their political and military ranks."

One director stood and began to applaud. Others joined him.

"We have accomplished our mission!" one director shouted. Others chimed in.

The white-haired man held up his hand to silence the room.

Shaking his head, the white-haired man responded, "No. There is much more we need to do."

"What more could you want?" the medical doctor questioned. "Much of the world is fighting disease, stock markets are plunging, unemployment is skyrocketing, and citizens are looting and fighting each other for food and supplies, countries are closing their borders and an attitude of isolationism has taken hold. We now have full power in manipulating markets to our financial advantage. That was our goal and we have accomplished it."

The directors sat in silence as they anticipated the white-haired man's response.

He let out a sigh then said, "I want more." He paused before continuing. His voice lowered and he spoke each word with intent. "This disruption in civil decency and international cooperation sets up the perfect environment for war." He paused again. "War, gentlemen, is when we see the most profits. War is when we attain the greatest power. And to succeed at war, we must have nuclear weapons."

"I object!" the medical director stood suddenly.

"I agree," the financial director added. "And it is clear that several other directors do as well. I propose that we end this meeting on the successful and positive outcome of the Panama Contagion and hold off any discussion of war and nuclear weapons until another day." He smiled and gestured for the medical director to sit down.

"Yes, I second that proposal," the medical director said as he took his seat.

While the majority of directors agreed to end the meeting with the discussion of the Panama Contagion, the medical director leaned over and whispered into the financial director's ear, "We need a private meeting with the others to discuss the removal of our senior director." The financial director nodded and replied back, "I'll handle it."

The meeting was adjourned and the directors stood to leave. Many shook hands congratulating each other on their successes. As they began to leave the boardroom, the white-haired man pulled the Foreigner aside.

"Wait a moment while I gather my things," he admonished the Foreigner, yet he smiled and waved as the last directors left.

The Foreigner wiped sweat from his face, fearful of the repercussions that awaited him.

"Sir," he held up his hands, "it's not my fault that the canal explosions did not . . ."

"Oh, stop whining," the white-haired man interrupted, shaking his head with disgust. "I don't care about that now. What I want from you—and I know you will be very good at this—is to track down that Yi fellow, the one responsible for all the damage to our operations, and I want you to kill him."

The Foreigner quickly nodded his head. "Yes, I've already had one run-in with him. Killing him is first on my agenda," the Foreigner replied.

"If you've already dealt with him, why didn't you kill him then?" the white-haired man's voice rose in anger.

"I wanted him to suffer," the Foreigner smiled awkwardly.

The white-haired man's voice calmed. "Very good. Then he knows what you are capable of." He took a deep breath and continued, "Furthermore, I want you to use Bao's connections in America to hunt down Yi's girlfriend—what was her name?"

"Sarah."

"Yes, Sarah, the Tibetan judge who aided Yi in Hainan. I want her brought to Harbin. I am sure she will fetch a high price on the slave market." He smiled at the thought, then nodded. "Yes, they will both suffer long and hard for the damage they have caused to the Net. And then I want them killed."

"That will be my greatest pleasure," the Foreigner sighed and again wiped the beads of perspiration—this time in delightful anticipation—from his forehead with his finely stitched linen handkerchief with the letter X in the corner.

A NOTE TO YOU, DEAR READER:

Thank you for reading this book. I hope you enjoyed it, along with books 1 and 2 in The Net thriller series. Because I am an independent author, your opinions and word-of-mouth recommendations to others are the lifeblood of my writing career. I very much appreciate your support. If you have enjoyed my books, please tell your friends, and consider writing a positive review. If you liked/disliked the book, or found errors, or you just want to share your thoughts on any of the stories or characters, please email me at dmcoffman@gmail.com and tell me. I would love to hear from you. I have made changes to at least one book because a reader found a flaw in a storyline. I'll even send you a free Net Conspiracy t-shirt for taking the time to write to me.

Were you able to ferret out the facts from the fiction in my books? Much of my writing is based on my experiences while living in China, traveling, and also the news. To learn more, please drop by my website at www.dmcoffman.com.

COMING SOON – Book 4 in The Net thriller series.

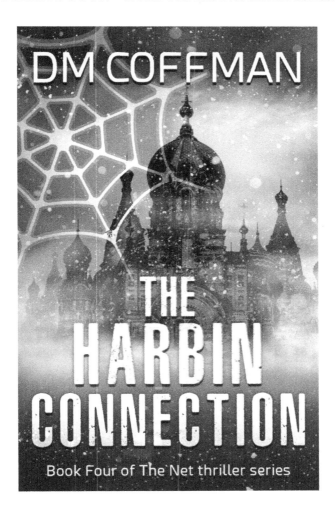

DM COFFMAN

THE HARBIN CONNECTION

Book Four of The Net thriller series

Author Biography

DM and her husband lived in the People's Republic of China for four years teaching with the World Trade Organization's China Judicial Training Program and Brigham Young University's China Teachers Program. Prior to living in China, DM and her husband worked in the legal profession in Washington, DC. Many experiences while in China inspired The Net thriller series, including DM being hospitalized with early SARS and the months it took to regain her health, having to travel wearing a face mask to return to the US, then being separated from her husband who was quarantined in Beijing.

DM Coffman specializes in clean quick read suspense thrillers. She is the author of The Net series including *The Net Conspiracy, The Hainan Conflict, The Panama Contagion,* and *The Harbin Connection* (coming soon). She also wrote the Whitney Award nominated suspense thriller *The Hainan Incident* published by Covenant Communications, Inc. which is an LDS version of the first two books in The Net thriller series. In non-fiction, she wrote *Above the Best: The Remarkable Life of Seeley E. Ralphs,* a biography, and *China Through the Eyes of Her Students* providing a glimpse at life in China through the uncensored writing journals of her students at Peking University and South China University of Technology. She also wrote *A Peking University Coursebook on English Exposition Writing,* published by Peking University Press, and she served as an editor and foreign consultant for English educational texts produced by China's Ministry of Education. She has a M.Ed. from Brigham Young University and a B.B.A. from National University.

Made in the USA
Monee, IL
06 December 2020